The Valentine's Day Disaster

By Lori Wilde

Somebody To Love
The Christmas Cookie Collection
All Out of Love
Love at First Sight
A Cowboy for Christmas
The Cowboy and the Princess
The Cowboy Takes a Bride
The Welcome Home Garden Club
The First Love Cookie Club
The True Love Quilting Club
The Sweethearts' Knitting Club

Available from Avon Impulse
The Valentine's Day Disaster
One True Love

THE CHRISTMAS COOKIE CHRONICLES:
Carrie
Raylene
Christine
Grace

The Valentine's Day Disaster

A TWILIGHT, TEXAS NOVELLA

LORI WILDE

AVON IMPULSE
An Imprint of HarperCollinsPublishers

An Excerpt from *Love With a Perfect Cowboy*. Copyright © 2014 by Laurie Vanzura.

An Excerpt from *The Last Wicked Scoundrel*. Copyright © 2014 by Jan Nowasky.

An Excerpt from *Blitzing Emily*. Copyright © 2014 by Julie Brannagh.

An Excerpt from *Savor*. Copyright © 2014 by Monica Murphy.

An Excerpt from *If You Only Knew*. Copyright © 2014 by Dixie Lee Brown.

EPub Edition FEBRUARY 2014 ISBN: 9780062311511

Print Edition ISBN: 9780062311528

10 9 8 7 6 5 4 3 2 1

The Valentine's Day Disaster

Chapter One

"QUESTION. HOW CAN anyone scowl so fiercely with a stage full of half-naked men parading around in front of her?" asked Jana Gerard.

Sesty Snow ironed her forehead with two fingers. Honestly? She wished she could skip right over the annual Twilight, Texas Valentine's Day celebration that now included the first ever Hunks-in-the-Hood bachelor auction.

The event—and the cutesy name—had been her own invention, but now she was stuck with it. Last summer she'd entered a hometown competition designed to spotlight local talent and create new events. It was designed to bring additional tourism dollars into Hood County and justify the new lakeside conference center that some gung-ho politico had convinced voters they needed.

One hundred entries, and winner, winner, chicken dinner, she'd beaten out them all.

At the time, peacock proud of herself, she collected the trappings of success. Renting office space on the town square for her fledgling event planning business. Buying her first home. Dating a hotshot lawyer.

But now?

Not so much.

However, she wasn't a quitter. Never had been, never would be. That is unless she counted pulling the plug on her relationship with Josh Langtree. She'd quit that easily enough.

Aw c'mon. Why was she thinking about Josh now? It had been almost ten years since she'd last seen him.

Why?

Well, the man *had* been her first love, and she was re-evaluating her life since getting dumped by said hotshot lawyer. Memory lane trips were de rigueur after breakups, were they not?

That, plus Josh had been all over the news lately, first crashing spectacularly in a NASCAR race in November and then getting dumped by his fashion model fiancée. Hey, they had something in common. Both of them were losers in the game of love.

When first she heard about his accident her impulse had been to call him and give condolences, but she had zero clue about how to get hold of him. No doubt he had bodyguards, and an entourage keeping the hoi polloi at bay.

Jana snapped her fingers in front of Sesty's face. "You stroke out on me or something?"

Sesty blinked. "Thanks for the heads-up on the scowling. I didn't realize I was doing that. I'm working on a headache. Getting these guys to listen to me is like herding stray cats stoned on peyote."

"Who's stoned on peyote?" Jana's sidelong glance sliced to the onstage studs, her lips softening into an expression Sesty thought best belonged behind closed doors, a sultry tilt of desire and seduction. "The cats or the herder?"

"Either or."

"Maybe both?" Jana swung her gaze back to Sesty. "Is something wrong?"

Jana was willow-branch thin and sported a zoo of colorful tattoos that included a parrot on her left shoulder, leopard spots across her chest, and exotic green serpents twining around her right leg. She wore a floral peasant skirt, ankle boots, and a short-waisted, brown leather jacket. Her eggplant-colored hair was clumped in dreadlocks, and numerous piercings punctuated her face. Two years ago she'd moved to Twilight from Austin, and the townspeople viewed her as something of a lovable oddity.

Sesty's parents had advised her against hiring Jana. "Image is important," they'd said. "Your assistant is an extension of you. She's far too Bohemian."

Secretly, a small rebellious part of her liked that Jana's appearance upset her parents. The girl was a damned good assistant, never mind her eccentricities, and that's all Sesty cared about.

"No, no, nothing's wrong." Sesty resisted the urge to sigh. "It's just that there's so much to do."

"I've never seen you this distracted no matter how much stress you're under. Something's up. What gives?"

"I'm fine," Sesty assured her, tucking her tablet computer under her arm and clapping her hands. "Ian Carter, could you please put down the cell phone for two minutes?"

Ian, the owner of the local jet-ski dealership and heart-attack-gorgeous, grinned a handsome-guys-can-get-away-with-anything grin and held up a finger. "Just one more text. I'm making V-Day dinner rez for me and my gal at the Funny Farm."

"Lucky girl." Jana breathed. "The food there is delicious, and the company . . ." She cast a roving eye over Ian's hard body and lowered her voice. "Let's just say if he didn't have a girlfriend, I'd hit that."

"Men." Sesty couldn't contain the sigh any longer. It slipped over her lips, soft and disappointed. "Why is he waiting until Wednesday to get a Friday reservation? He'll never get in."

"Of course he will. Ian's young, good-looking, and he can bribe people with free Sea-Doo rides."

"True, but I wish they'd listen to me for two minutes. You'd think the lot of them have ADHD."

"Seriously, Ses, do you even have a pulse? Who cares if they listen? Just look at them." Jana swept a hand at the men in various stages of undress, from Ian in a skintight wet suit, to a cowboy in boots, chaps, and tight-fitting jeans and nothing else, to the fireman in turnout gear, sans shirt.

"Since I'm the one who is responsible for putting on a seamless bachelor auction. I care. I care a lot."

"Your perfectionism is showing. You gotta learn to chill a little or you will stroke out before you're fifty."

What was so bad about striving to always do your best? Why did people consider it such a character flaw?

It was the same thing Chad said to her two weeks ago when he asked for the key to his place back. He also said she was overly cautious, uptight, and provincial. Sesty notched her chin up. If expecting monogamy from your boyfriend of three months was provincial, then yes, yes, she was. Guilty as charged.

"You demand too much of people," Chad had said. "Your expectations are too high."

Of course, it turned out to be a bullshit excuse. She learned he was slipping around behind her back with the leggy bimbo who ran Perks, the new coffee shop on the square.

Dammit. She was going to miss her morning cup of mocha latte more than she would miss Chad. Why couldn't he have taken up with the woman who owned the sports memorabilia store? She never jonesed for a Hank Aaron autographed baseball.

To rub salt in the wound, Chad had delivered this parting shot: "You think you're so perfect, but you're not. You're just a control freak who you can't ever let go, and quite frankly, that makes you a washout in the sack."

Oh yeah, that last bit had stung, even more than his betrayal. She tried so hard to be a good lover. She read sex manuals and bought sexy lingerie, really worked at it. The only time sex had come naturally to her had been with . . . well, never mind that.

Sesty swallowed the bitter taste in her mouth and said

to Jana, "What you call perfectionism, I call organization. It's gotten me this far. I'm sticking with it."

"There's organized and then there's you." Jana chuckled.

Fine. She would own it. She loved files and spreadsheets and color-coded tabbed folders, any and everything that smacked of orderliness. What kind of event planner would she be if she weren't organized?

"Leaving the topic of my faults for the time being, we've got a week's worth of work and three days to do it in." Sesty pushed her bangs from her forehead and puffed out her cheeks with air.

This year, Valentine's Day was on Friday, so Twilight was doing what they did best—making a big production out of holidays, and stealing the entire weekend from Saint Valentine. Her bachelor auction was the linchpin of Saturday's activities, which included a dress-up-your-pet-as-a-famous-lover-from-film contest, a dulcimer competition, wine-tasting featuring Texas vintners, some romance author having a book signing and for the kids, and a smashing of the giant heart-shaped piñata in the town square.

One eyebrow shot up on Jana's forehead. "When you hired me, you told me that Valentine's Day was your favorite holiday. Now it seems like you're gritting your teeth to get through this."

Once upon a time, Valentine's Day *had* been her favorite holiday. What wasn't to love about flowers and chocolates and heartfelt expressions of love?

But that was before.

"All right." Sesty folded her arms over her chest and ignored Jana's question. "There *is* one problem. These uncooperative men are driving me batty. We need to get this dress rehearsal over with and be out of the building by one o'clock so the vendors can start setting up for the bridal show on Friday."

"You're not going to tell me what's eating you, are you?"

"Nothing's eating me."

"Fine. Keep your secrets." Jana stuck two fingers in her mouth and let loose with a long, loud whistle. "Yo, dudes, total attention over here." She swirled a finger above Sesty's head.

The men migrated to the edge of the stage, stared out to where she and Jana stood in front of the auditorium seating.

"Thank you all for volunteering," Sesty addressed them. "All the proceeds from the auction will go to Holly's House, a charity that helps provide medical care to needy families in Hood County. I know you are busy men so we'll keep this rehearsal as short as possible. If you'd line up along the stage in the order listed on your instruction sheet that would be very helpful."

The gorgeous men, in various stages of undress, obeyed. All right, so she was no longer keen on Valentine's Day, but she had to admit the masculine eye candy was tonic for her bruised ego.

She surveyed the bachelors, did a head count. "One, two, three. Scott, Mitchell, Dickie. Four, five, six . . ." Hey wait, there were only eleven bachelors. She turned to

Jana. "We're missing one. There's supposed to be twelve. Where's number twelve?"

"Didn't I tell you?" It was Jana's turn to scowl. "I thought I told you. I know I told you."

"No, you didn't tell me."

Jana's nose crinkled. "I meant to tell you. Gray Kemper had to drop out of the auctions for health reasons."

As a former minor league pitcher for a Texas Rangers farm team, Gray was expected to bring in the most money.

"What health reasons?" People had a habit of committing to something and then backing out when the time drew near. She wasn't going to let Gray weasel out of his commitment over a minor illness.

"He ruptured his Achilles' tendon playing basketball."

"Ouch." Sesty winced. "Oh, okay, good excuse, but I promised Holly's House twelve bachelors. We need twelve bachelors. Thank heavens we haven't printed the programs yet. Who can we draft as Gray's stand-in at this late date?"

"I've already been searching around," Jana assured her. "But it's not like hunky bachelors are falling from the sky or anything. Most of the good-looking, single guys in Twilight are already up there on stage."

Another hurdle.

Sesty took a deep breath. Fine. She could handle this. Troubleshooting was one of her strengths. "There's six thousand people in Granbury. Assuming the law of averages, half of them have to be men."

"Don't forget we have a big retiree population. Unless you want to feature the Grampas of Hood County."

"Well, monkey pudding." Sesty sank her hands on

her hips, tablet computer still tucked under her armpit. "What now?"

"We could settle for an ordinary looking guy. Not every guy has to be a literal hunk. We could go for hunky personalities. I bet Linc over at the feed store would do it."

Sesty tapped her chin with the knuckle of her second finger. "Linc is a sweet guy, but he perpetually smells of medicated livestock feed and he's six-foot-eight."

"Choosy beggar."

"Is there anyone else you can think of?"

"There's always Chad, if you don't mind someone bidding on a date with your main squeeze."

Eek. Sesty gulped. She'd rather go down to the Horny Toad Tavern, yank any random drunk off a bar stool and stick him on the stage before stooping so low as to ask Chad for help.

The men were getting restless again, taking out cell phones, rehashing the Super Bowl, pantomiming boxing each other. She suppressed an eye roll. Men. Underneath, they were all thirteen at heart. She'd better stop worrying about the one that was missing and corral the eleven she had on hand.

Jana was right. She was procrastinating. Why?

Valentine's Day. The fault lay with the silly day that honored the schmaltzy, mushy side of love.

Forget Valentine's Day.

Right. Okay. Head in the game.

From behind her, she heard the main door of the conference center creak open, and a rectangle of sunlight spilled across the stage. She didn't turn to see who'd come in. Mostly likely it was a local woman or two creeping inside to check out the hunks. She didn't mind. Nothing wrong with stirring grassroots buzz about the guys. Just as long as visitors didn't disrupt rehearsal, they were welcome to stay.

"Linc it is then," she murmured to Jana, and then to the men she said, "Fellas, if you could—"

"Uh, Ses." Jana plucked at the sleeve of Sesty's angora sweater.

"What is it?" she asked without glancing over at her assistant.

"Mmm, don't look now, but I think a miracle might have just strolled through the door."

"Huh?" Slowly, Sesty swiveled her head.

A man stood in the doorway, backlit by the noonday sun and letting in the crisp February air. His face was cast in shadow and she could not make out his features, but his body—from what she could see at this distance—well . . . ahem . . . he put every other man up on that stage to shame.

"I'm looking for Jana Gerard," he called out. "Marge from the courthouse sent me over."

"Down here." Jana waved wildly.

That voice. It was eerily familiar to Sesty. Hot chills rippled across her chest and her scalp tingled. Did she know him?

The man ambled closer, moving like a well-fed cougar idly scoping out a herd of cattle for future reference— leisurely, relaxed, but ever watchful. The closer he got, the harder Sesty's heart pounded. His pace was casual but controlled. It dawned on her that he was struggling not to limp. As the door clicked closed behind him, blocking out the sunlight, his features came into sharp focus.

She knew all six feet two inches of him. Those angular lips had once kissed her. Those muscled arms had once held her. Those sharp eyes had drilled through her more times than she could count.

His chestnut-colored hair was longer than it had been in high school. It lay in tousled waves, and her fingers itched to comb through the thick, lush locks. Underneath his open black leather jacket, a black, waffle-weave, button-down thermal shirt stretched across a chest that was broader, sturdier, than she remembered. Faded Levi's sat low on his hips and a pair of black motorcycle boots shod his feet.

"Josh Langtree," she whispered.

He gave her a front cover of *Sports Illustrated* smile. "You remembered."

As if she could forget the first guy who'd ever made love to her. A guy who was now a NASCAR star. Her head spun dizzily and she realized she was holding her breath.

Breathe.

But she wasn't the only one who recognized him. Immediately, the eleven bachelors bailed off stage, crowding around Josh, pounding him on the back, bumping fists, slapping high-fives, hooting and hollering and doing all that testosterone-dripping stuff men did when adulating a returning conqueror.

"Oh, brother," she muttered under her breath.

"Yo!" Jana clapped her hands. "Hate to break up the

bro-fest, but we're on the clock here. You can worship at his feet later." Making wide shooing motions, she herded the men back up on stage.

Leaving Sesty alone with Josh.

"Zesty Sesty," he drawled. "Twice as beautiful and sexier than ever."

Instantly, Sesty's cheeks burned hot as a pancake griddle. The old words he used to tease her with. *Zesty Sesty.*

"You're back in town," she said, because she didn't know what else to say.

"I am."

"Wh-Wh-What . . ." *Oh, for godsakes, spit it out.* "What are you doing here?"

"Came home to recover after my accident. Maybe you heard about it?"

There was a note in his tone—part hopeful, part sad, part braggy, part lonely—that yanked at something inside her.

Of course she'd heard about it. The spectacular crash had been on TV and was the talk of the town for a good week. In fact, she'd watched horrified until they pulled him from the wreckage and he jumped to his feet, arms clasped over his head in a victory-over-death gesture that had made her mad. His dangerous antics had been the very thing that broke them up. She'd been unable to tolerate the fear that came with loving a daredevil.

For the first time, she noticed the fresh scar at the hollow of his throat. His injuries had been bad enough to require a tracheotomy? That conflicted with what she'd seen on TV and heard in media reports. Her stomach contracted and a sick feeling spread over her. What had happened?

"It's not really an accident when you choose to drive a car at two hundred miles an hour," she popped off, fear taking possession of her tongue, and saying something snarky when more than anything she wanted to wrap her arms around him and tell him how happy she was that he survived. "Death wish might be a better word."

"Actually." His grin ribbed her. "That's two words."

"It's still foolhardy any way you slice it. Grown men speeding around a track trying to prove who has the most testosterone."

"Ten years and you still can't let it go, can you?"

The men on stage were calling to him, throwing out a hundred questions about NASCAR. Great. Just great. She was swiftly losing control. Which always happened when Josh Langtree was around.

She straightened. "I meant what are you doing here at our dress rehearsal?"

"Judge Blackthorne sent me."

"Why would Judge Blackthorne send you to me?"

He lowered his eyelids. "Helping you is part of my community service commitment."

"Community service?" She wet her lips. "What did you do?"

"Long story. The upshot is you're stuck with me for forty hours. The judge said you're in need of hands and feet."

It took a couple of heartbeats for her to absorb this. Josh Langtree was not only back in town, but he was at her service? Just when she was in desperate need of a sexy bachelor. It seemed perfect, but it felt like a trap.

He held his palms out wide. "So here I am. Hands and feet. What can I do for you?"

She hesitated only a second and then blurted, "Strip off your shirt."

Chapter Two

STRIP OFF YOUR SHIRT.

If they had been all alone in the conference center, Sesty's words would have sounded like Ravel's *Bolero* to Josh's ears and he would have popped the buttons off his shirt in a mad rush to get naked for her.

Under the circumstances, however . . .

He used his hand as a stop sign. "Oh no. I'm here to help tote and carry, not star in this little dog and pony show."

"We're short a bachelor. You've got community service to work out. Looks like you don't have much of a choice. Or maybe I should call Judge Blackthorne." Her grin made a clean threat. Not a tolerant grin; not a teasing grin; not even a pissed off grin, just taking a stand and meaning it.

Damn but she looked so damn sexy with those Queen-of-the-Nile cheekbones and lush full lips. Not overtly, like she was trying too hard, but an innate inner sexiness that she wasn't even aware of. Girl-next-door stuff. On the strength of that grin, he had an urge to sell his home in Houston and move back to Twilight for good.

Except he'd shaken the dust off his tires and zoomed away from this sleepy burg a long time ago. Even coming here to recover felt like he was moving in reverse.

"You've got a cruel streak, Snow. Anyone ever tell you that?"

"Shirt." She snapped her fingers at him. "Off."

Momentarily, he thought about refusing. She'd always been a little bossy. Not that he minded. He liked a woman who knew her own mind.

She appraised him with cool indigo eyes, daring him to chicken out. Fine. If that's how she wanted to play it, he would embarrass the living fire out of her. Slowly, he slipped out of his leather jacket, dropped it onto one of the auditorium seats, and then reached for the top button of his shirt.

Her eyes were hooked on his fingers, tracking his every move.

The V-neck sweater she wore, red as Valentine's Day, clung to her magnificent breasts and revealed just a hint of superb cleavage. Low-rise, snug-fitting black-denim jeans hugged curvy hips. Her hair was caught back with a brown leather strap, but wild tendrils of honey blond strands had escaped to float around her face. Brick. Freaking. House.

A refrain from an old song, "You Dropped a Bomb on Me," ran through his head. Boom! He could almost smell gunpowder.

He lowered his eyelids, shot her a smoldering stare, and flicked open the second button of his shirt.

She licked her lips, swallowed visibly, but she did not glance away.

That was his Sesty. Brave as hell, even if she didn't think it of herself.

Too damn bad they were in a roomful of people. A decade had passed since the last time he'd seen her, but it could have been ten minutes. She looked exactly the same. Correction, she looked even better than she had at seventeen—filled out in all the right places, flawless skin, go-getter set to her shoulders. Time had been very generous to Sesty Snow.

He reached the last button and his shirt gaped open. He worked out with weights three times a week. A race-car driver's life might seem sedentary, but the sport required a high level of fitness. You had to be able to react quickly, both mentally and physically. A sharp mind required a sharp body.

The doctors told him that if he hadn't been in such great physical shape, he wouldn't have pulled through the complications following the crash, after he had an anaphylactic reaction to a drug he didn't know he was allergic to. Somehow, his publicist managed to keep that out of the media.

The heated sheen in her eyes made all his time at the gym worth the effort. Josh shrugged out of the shirt and tossed it to her.

She caught it one-handed, her eyes growing to the size of Oreos and her cheeks blooming the color of pink cotton candy.

She'd always blushed easily, and he'd bet his right thumb she was seriously regretting that "strip off your shirt" line.

He couldn't help puffing out his chest. *You asked for it baby, you got it.*

Sesty closed her eyes but then opened them quickly. The blush was fading, but her pupils were still as big as quarters.

He flexed a bicep. "What do you think?"

"You'll do." She tried to appear unimpressed, but the pulse at the hollow of her throat was pumping like a piston.

"Even with my bum knee?"

"You hide it well enough."

"Thanks. I've been working on it. Takes time."

"How long have you been back in Twilight?" she asked, restlessly drumming her fingers against that smart little chin. God, he'd forgotten how cute she was.

"Couple of days." Josh flicked his gaze to her fingers.

"This is the first time you've been home since you left? Why are you back now?"

"My doctor told me to get away from the city. Relax. Heal."

"Tall order for you. Exchanging excitement and action for peace and quiet."

He shrugged like it was water off his back, but he knew that she saw straight through him. Sesty had always seen through his bravado in a way no one else ever had. It was weird being back home with the woman who knew him better than he knew himself.

"It must be tough." Sympathy softened her face. "Sitting on the sidelines while the NASCAR season starts up without you."

"The show must go on," he murmured.

"You'll soon be back in the game," she assured him.

"I'm not sure I want to be."

"What?" Her eyes widened in disbelief. "Why not?"

"A fella comes that close to dying, it changes the way he thinks about things."

She raised a hand to her throat. "I hadn't realized your accident was that severe. I saw you hop from the wreckage—"

"You watched the race?" Damn, why did he have to so sound so eager?

"No," she admitted. "I caught the replay on the news. You were the talk of Twilight."

"Ah yeah, hometown boy does good, and then it all goes horribly wrong."

"What happened? Or do you hate talking about it?"

Yes, he hated talking about it. The wreck had not been his finest hour. His cocky self-confidence had gotten the better of him. His crew chief, Hal Penser was feeding him moves through the headset, but his instincts had told him that Hal's advice was wrong. If he wanted to win, he had to do the exact opposite maneuver than the one his advisor suggested. And his plan would have worked too, except he hadn't counted on the car in front of him throwing a tire at exactly the wrong moment.

But hey, if he'd listened to his crew chief, he wouldn't have had a prayer of winning the race. Then again he would not have crashed so spectacularly either. *Gotta take some risks to achieve great glory,* was what he told Hal when the crew chief came to see him in the hospital. Hal shot back that dead men didn't have much use for glory.

"What do you want from me now?" he asked, letting Sesty's question lie there unanswered. "The shirt's off."

"Um . . . um . . ." She moistened her lips again, her pink tongue flicking out quickly, unintentionally provocative. Did she still taste like pears poached in white wine—sweet, light, and intoxicating? "Get up on the stage with the others."

"Yes, ma'am," he drawled. Meandering to control the twinge in his right knee, he moved toward the stage without a backward glance, although he was pretty sure she was staring at his ass. He hadn't realized how much he missed her until he saw her again.

None of that, Langtree.

He had enough problems without adding Sesty to the mix. Never mind that his mouth burned to taste her again and his fingers tingled at the thought of combing through that silky thicket of honey blond hair.

What was going on here? Two months ago, a convenient few weeks after his accident, his fiancée had left him for his best friend. He had to hand it to her. Miley sure had perfect timing. She really knew how to kick a man when he was on the ground.

Yep. Josh was finished with love. From now on he was a lone wolf. Sex, oh sure. He'd still have plenty of that, but love? No more. It was not worth the pain. Which meant not lusting after his high school sweetheart. Because Sesty wasn't the type of woman you could simply have sex with and then just walk away. He'd done it once and it had about killed him.

Josh reached the end of the line of men standing on stage, took his place next to the firefighter in his turn-out gear and pivoted on his heel to face forward. Sesty was addressing the first bachelor, directing him where to stand during the auction, but Josh didn't miss the fact that she kept throwing furtive glances his way.

He wasn't in this alone. She felt it too. The heat. The sizzle. That old magic. He throttled up his grin. They had been damned good together.

But hey, things changed. Right? He wasn't the same cocky kid who sped away from Twilight with stars in his eyes and big dreams on his mind. He was certain she'd changed too.

He studied her impeccable profile. That fluffy sweater was soft and inviting, and it had slipped down her shoulder a little, revealing a bit of bra strap.

Black.

She was wearing a black bra. Looking at her made him ache in all the right places.

Or wrong places, depending on how you looked at it.

Why was it they had broken up in the first place? Oh yeah, she said she needed a man she could count on, not a daredevil intent on getting himself killed.

Had she found what she was looking for? He shifted his gaze to her left hand. No ring on that third finger.

Since his family had moved from Twilight nine years

ago, he hadn't been back to town, didn't really keep up with any of his old high school friends. He had no idea what she'd been up to, but suddenly he had a desperate need to find out.

Ice it, Langtree. You've got no chance with her. You don't want a chance with her. Remember?

Yeah, that sounded good, but his body wasn't all that interested in walking away. In fact, just watching her had him growing embarrassingly hard.

Sesty trotted them through their paces, insisting each bachelor prove he wouldn't stumble or fumble come auction day. She was so fierce, so intent, her eyes blazing with the fire of her job. The woman loved what she did for a living. He could see it on her.

When rehearsal was over and Sesty had dismissed the bachelors, Josh was surprised to discover that the last thing he wanted to do was leave. When Judge Blackthorne handed down his community service sentence, he felt doomed, but that was before he knew Sesty was in charge of this shindig.

Zesty Sesty. He sure missed teasing her.

And looking at her.

Everyone else filed from the building, including Sesty's funky-looking assistant. Sesty was busy collecting her things. He eased down off the stage and ambled toward her, his pulse picking up the closer he got. He had not expected to feel like this, as if he was seventeen all over again.

"You wanna grab something to drink?" he asked, surprised at how breathless he sounded.

"I'm not thirsty," she said primly, her slender shoulders going as stiff as her upper lip.

"A bite to eat, then?"

"Not hungry either." Her stomach growled. Loudly.

Josh lowered his head. "That's not what your belly says."

She pressed a hand to her solar plexus. "I'm fine."

"When did you last eat?"

"I had breakfast." Her nose wrinkled. "I think."

"You don't know whether you ate or not?"

"I've got a lot on my mind." She waved a dismissive hand. "I can't remember inconsequential details."

"Like food."

"I'm not going to die if I skip a meal or two."

"Maybe not," he said, "but you look sensational. Woman like you . . ." He shook his head. "You're not built to be a skinny-mini. Don't fight nature. Forget the strict diets and just eat good healthy food."

"Thanks for your unsolicited advice on my eating habits. I'm not trying to lose weight. I've been too busy to think about food." She didn't glance up from the tablet computer she was frantically using one-finger keyboarding to tap notes into.

"I can see why Judge Blackthorne sent me over here. You definitely need some help. Gotta stop lighting the candles at both ends or you'll flame out." He took the tablet from her hand.

"Hey! What are you doing?"

"Taking you to lunch."

"I can't, Josh, I've got too much too do," she protested. "Please give me my iPad back."

He held the device out of her reach. "And you can't do anything well without fueling your body."

"I'll grab something from a vending machine. Eat on the go. I do it all the time."

"That's junk, not fuel. Besides, sitting down to a meal will help you relax."

"Not if I'm sitting across from *you*," she mumbled.

"Ah-ha." He chuckled. She as good as admitted he knocked her off-kilter.

"No ah-ha. There's not an ah-ha here." She glared.

"You're confessing that I stir you up."

She snorted indelicately. "No. You haven't stirred me up in over a decade."

He tipped his chin up. "But once upon a time?"

"Check your ego at the door, Langtree. We were an item for about ten minutes in high school. You didn't make *that* big of an impression on me."

"That's not how I remember it," he said, lowering his voice. "As I recall, you walked into a wall on my first day when I transferred to Twilight High because you were too busy staring at me to watch where you were going."

"I did not!" she denied. The pink flush was back, spreading up her long, slender neck. He'd rattled her cage.

"And when my parents hired you to tutor me in English—"

"I was dismayed with you, not impressed."

"But later . . . you were impressed."

"I barely remember."

"We dated for six months."

"Ten minutes in the grand scheme of life, and that's being generous."

"If you want your tablet back you have to come to lunch with me." He waggled the minicomputer over her head.

"That's blackmail."

"So it is."

"All right, if I do go eat lunch with you, then you have to spend the rest of the afternoon helping me build the sets for the bachelor auction."

Such punishment. Spending the afternoon working side-by-side with his gorgeous high school sweetheart. Oh the pain.

He had her right where he wanted her. Yes, he might have sworn off love, but sex was another matter entirely. And all he could think about was how hot Sesty would look stretched out naked over his sheets.

"You'll write it up as my community service hours?" he bargained, not wanting to seem too eager to be alone with her. It was dangerous to let a woman know how much you wanted her.

"I will."

He handed back her tablet, but when her hand closed over the computer, he held on tight.

"What is it now?" She tapped an impatient foot.

"Just one more thing."

She rolled her eyes. "I knew it. Nothing is ever straightforward with you, is it? What's the thing?"

"We have to sit in a dark corner in the back of the restaurant."

"No." She tugged on the tablet, but he clung on. "I'm not doing anything romantic."

"Who said anything about romance? I just don't want our meal interrupted by autograph seekers."

"Oh," she said, and looked embarrassed.

"You thought I wanted to—"

"No I didn't."

"Look, my only objective is to feed you and catch up with your life." *And see if you're receptive to a fun fling for old times' sake.*

She raised a suspicious eyebrow. "And that's it?"

He held up two fingers. "Scout's honor."

"You were never a scout. They wouldn't let you in."

"Gotta admit it sounds better than scoundrel's honor."

That drew a but-you-are-a-scoundrel-aren't-you smile out of her, and he released his grip on her tablet.

"Thank you," she said, and tucked the computer into her handbag.

"Let's go." He extended his elbow toward her. "I'm starving."

She hesitated a moment, but then slipped her arm though his. The second her delicate hand hooked around his elbow, Josh realized he had made a major mistake.

Whether she knew it or not, Sesty still had him by the short hairs, and that was a damn scary notion.

Chapter Three

THEY SETTLED ON Pasta Pappa's, a cozy little Italian restaurant on the square. In keeping with her promise, Sesty agreed to a table in the far corner of the room that was situated behind a faux ficus plant, shielding them from full view of the most of the restaurant patrons.

On the walk over they were stopped several times by NASCAR fans and autograph seekers. Josh was gracious and generous with his time, but it took them a good twenty minutes to walk two blocks.

The waitress was all flutter at serving Josh Langtree and begged for a picture, which she promptly texted to everyone in the address book of her smart phone. Okay, Sesty told herself, no eye-rolling at fan girl here. When the waitress finally settled down, Josh ordered a Greek salad with grilled chicken; Sesty went for a meatball calzone. Giggling and winking at Josh, the waitress departed.

Was this how his entire life went?

Sesty scooted back in the spindly-legged wooden chair, trying to get some distance. She couldn't stop thinking about just how stomach-dropping hot he looked without his shirt on. The man was going to bring a pretty penny on the auction block. Guaranteed.

When she woke up that morning, if anyone had told her she'd be having lunch with her ex–high school sweetheart turned NASCAR star, she would have laughed at the ridiculousness of the idea. But here she was, feeling tongued-tied and weirdly jealous of all the women in the restaurant craning their necks for a better look at him.

Why did she care? He was no longer hers. Hadn't been for a decade.

Josh leaned back and studied her through half-closed eyelids.

She cradled her elbows in her palms and admired the healthy green of the ficus. Real or plastic? He was still staring at her. *Ulp.* Why did her head feel like wispy summer clouds whenever she looked at him?

It was suddenly too quiet, in spite of the din of voices, clanking silverware, and piped-in Italian mood music, "That's Amore." At the moment, she'd much rather hear J. Geils Band's "Love Stinks."

Along with the red and white checkered tablecloth and the basket-wrapped Chianti bottle with a white candle half burned down that was so clichéd. She almost expected to look up and see Lady and her Tramp chewing on the same strand of spaghetti.

Not to mention the added cheese factor of Valentine's Day decor. Paper hearts on bright red string dangled from the exposed beam rafters. A chubby-face, papier-mâché Cupid, arrow drawn, swung on a chain above their head in the blast from the heater vents. At the cash register, instead of the usual mints, sat a bowl of Be Mine heart candy.

This was her hometown. Always milking the romantic angle for the tourist trade.

She shoved her brain into overdrive, searching for something neutral to say, and came up with, "Where are you staying?"

"Why? Are you offering to let me stay with you?" His tone was light and teasing, the same glib tone he'd used on the waitress.

"No."

"I was afraid of that." He reached for a bread stick from the basket the waitress had deposited in the middle of the table when they first arrived, broke it in half. The bread stick snapped, crisp and clean.

"You thought you'd just swagger into town and I'd fall into bed with you?"

"A guy can hope, right?" He winked slow and sexy.

"Your breath? Don't hold it."

He inhaled deeply, expanding that beautiful broad chest. His eyes latched onto hers and the look robbed all the air from her body. They sat there, not breathing together. Her lungs burned. Head throbbed. She curled her hands into fists against the tabletop, tried to fight the urgent need for oxygen.

Josh interlaced his fingers, reached them back to cup his head in his palms, elbows sticking out beyond his ears. He looked as if he could go on like this for hours.

Finally, she was forced to gulp in a hungry breath.

He broke into an I-win grin, dropped his arms and exhaled.

"Showoff," she panted.

"You were going to lose from the start. I run sprints."

"Braggart."

"To answer your question, I'm staying at my grand-mother's old place over on Pike Street. The renters moved out at the end of January and the house needs some up-dating. I promised my folks I'd handle it."

"How are your parents?"

"Loving retirement and being full-time RVers. They come to all my races."

"They were there when you crashed?"

"Yeah," he said. "Downside of having them in the stands."

"It's sweet that they're so supportive."

"They weren't always. They were on your side. Thought I should buckle down, go to college. Make something of myself. They didn't understand how being dyslexic made college pure torture for me."

"Looks like you found your calling."

He made a self-deprecating noise. "It doesn't last for-ever."

The forlorn expression on his face had her wanting to reach across the table to lay her hand on his, but she re-sisted the urge. "Is your career in jeopardy?"

He flashed a nothing-gets-me-down grin, but it wa-vered, not fully reaching his eyes. "Hell, no."

Had the wreck taken some of the wildness out of him?

His impulsive, balls-to-the-wall attitude was one of the things that had attracted her to him. She was always so careful, so in control, that being near him had given her a thrill. But his recklessness had also terrified her, and it was the main reason she broke up with him. Thrills were great for the short term, but a lifetime of roller coaster rides would take its toll. Even at seventeen she understood that.

"I'm sorry," she said.

"Why? It's not your fault."

"I don't like seeing you suffer."

He didn't say anything for the longest moment, just watched her.

She squirmed.

"Why should you care?" he asked.

"I care about all my former boyfriends." She wasn't about to admit she still had lingering feelings for him. Might as well hand him a loaded gun and aim it at her heart.

"All?" He sounded amused. "How many old boyfriends did you have?"

"Scads," she lied.

Three.

She'd had exactly three steady boyfriends in her twenty-seven years on the planet, but he did not need to know that. Three lovers, and he'd been one of them. Yes, she'd dated plenty, but had never been able to do casual relationships like a lot of her friends. They teased her about it. Called her a dinosaur. But to Sesty, sex meant something. If you gave it away to everyone who halfway struck a spark in you, sex lost its significance.

"Scads, huh?" He appeared relaxed to the casual observer, slumped back as he was, legs extended, arm draped loosely over the arm of his chair, but Sesty knew him. She could read the telltale signs, the tension in his jaw, the smile that did not reach his eyes. Was he jealous?

"Scads," she confirmed.

"And yet, out of the hordes, you're here with me."

She traced a finger along the hem seam of the white cloth napkin spread across her lap. "Only because you blackmailed me into having lunch with you."

"True that. Now you don't have to feel sorry for me."

"Does it bother you?" she asked. "That I feel sorry for you?"

"Yeah. Pity is not a turn-on."

"That's perfect." She sat up straighter. "Since it's not my intention to turn you on."

"Honey," he drawled, and ogled her as if she were stark naked. "It doesn't matter what you want, not as long as you're sitting there looking good enough to eat."

Her pulse fluttered through her veins, a crazy butterfly with nothing better to do than flap its mindless wings. *Don't let him see that he's getting to you.* "You haven't changed a bit. Still full of b.s."

"To hell with me. Let's talk about you." He scooted his chair closer, leaned in.

She shivered.

"Cold?" He reached around, whipping his leather jacket off the back of the chair. Before she could tell him that she was fine, he was on his feet and swathing his jacket around her shoulders. "There."

"Thanks," she whispered as his scent enveloped her. His jacket smelled so familiar—leather and licorice and Lava soap.

He sat back down. "So how did you end up in charge of this Valentine's Day show?"

She let out a long, slow breath and told him the details of starting her own event planning business, entering the contest, winning it.

His eyes widened. "That's impressive."

"You sound surprised."

"Not surprised. I just thought you were so tied into your family that you'd eventually be running the Sweetheart Inn yourself. You always were the most organized person I ever met."

She thrust out her jaw. "There's nothing wrong with being organized."

"I never said there was.

"You used to," she said. "Complain about my organizational skills."

"Did I?"

"You said I overscheduled my life. Tried too hard to toe the line." She'd heard the very same criticism from Chad two weeks ago.

He plucked a brown packet of turbinado sugar from the holder on the table and toyed with it, turning the packet around in his tanned fingers. "And you said I was too impulsive."

Sesty pushed her bangs off her forehead. "We were young."

"And dumb."

"*Really* dumb."

His eyes turned obsidian, dark and bottomless, and a flood of heat rushed to her pelvis. "Do you regret it, Ses?"

"What?" she whispered, every muscle in her body tightened.

"Me being your first?"

Her heart staggered across her chest so dramatically, it barely registered that the waitress had settled their food in front of them. Why was he bringing up ancient history? "I'm beginning to regret this lunch."

"Am I making you uncomfortable?"

"Not at all," she said blithely. "But I'm a busy woman. I don't have time for idle chitchat."

"The reason I ask . . ." He leaned back. ". . . is that I'm in the process of reevaluating my life."

"Deep thoughts?" Her muscles were rocks now. "That's unlike you."

"I'm backtracking, trying to see how I've screwed up the relationships in my life."

"Really, really deep thoughts. If you were in AA, I'd say you were on step nine. Are you in AA?"

He snorted. "No. I don't even drink."

She leaned forward until hers arms touched the table. "That wreck must have done a number on you."

"There's more to it than that."

She cocked her head and waited for him to continue, unable to believe he was opening up to her like this. Like most men she knew, Josh had never been one to talk about his feelings. She knew he must be going through something heavy duty.

"I was engaged," he said.

"I heard about that. What happened?"

He winced. "So clichéd it could have been a country and western song. I caught her in bed with my best friend."

She put a hand to her heart. "Oh, Josh."

"No, no." He waggled a finger. "No more pity. Even though I didn't realize it at the time, it was for the best."

"Still, getting cheated on like that." She shook her head, pushed the tip of her tongue against the inside of her upper lip. "Kick in the gut."

"Ironic," he said, "that I'm seriously down on love in general and Valentine's Day in particular, and here I am, forced to sell myself at a Valentine's Day bachelor auction to the highest bidder. I imagine God is having a good laugh at my expense."

She really didn't want to hear about his ex. "So community service. What's that all about?"

"Oh that." An embarrassed expression sent his eyebrows up and his mouth sideways. "I'm not proud of myself."

"But . . . ?"

"I took issue with my grandmother's next-door neighbor's Valentine's Day display."

"Miss Pendergarten does tend to go a bit overboard." She let out her breath, felt her body unwind as the topic shifted.

"Overboard?" Josh snorted. "Understatement of the century. Love songs playing on outdoor speakers all night long. Red heart twinkle lights strung from the eaves. Six-foot-tall, cherry red, neon lips on her front lawn that blink in my bedroom window at three o'clock in the morning bright enough to damage my retinas."

"Her decorations are pretty garish. What did you do?" Sesty took a bite of her calzone. Chewed.

"I tried talking to her like a reasonable person—"

"If Miss Pendergarten feels threatened, she has a tendency to get irrational and aggressive. You threatened her outlook on love."

"Is that what I did?"

"She's got borderline personality disorder. She's needy."

"Now you tell me."

"Do you also know that she's Judge Blackthorne's half sister?"

"Yeah, I found that out too late."

"Exactly what did you do?" Sesty prodded.

He held up his palms as if she'd drawn a gun on him. "It was self-protection. I didn't mean for it to turn out the way it did, but at three in the morning I wasn't thinking all that clearly."

"Things are always worse at three in the morning. "Did you take a hatchet to her decorations or something?"

"Now that's a thought, but no, I'm not malicious. Even at three in the morning. I know how much she loves her schmaltz. I just wanted to get some sleep, so I slipped over there to unplug the blinking lips."

"You got community service for that? Where's the crime?"

"Trespassing, for one thing, but wait." He licked his index finger and raised it in the air. "It gets worse."

"I can just see you creeping onto Miss Pendergarten's

lawn in the middle of the night." She couldn't help firing him a breezy grin.

"You're going to laugh at my humiliation?"

"Sorry." She curled her lips around her teeth to keep from smiling. "Go on."

"I sneaked over there and located the electrical plug, but apparently I wasn't the only one with an anti–Valentine's Day sentiment, because she had already rigged an alarm system to the damn things."

"Uh-oh."

"Yeah. When the alarm went off, I jumped a foot, and with my bum knee . . ."

"Ouch."

"I fell against the lips, knocked them over, and they busted against the flagstone walkway. Miss P comes shrieking out of the house dressed like Lily Munster. What's that all about, by the way? And acting like I backed over her cat or something."

"Sounds like Miss Pendergarten, all right." Sesty nodded. "She favors gauzy gowns. She used to be an actress. Just local stuff mostly. Her biggest success when she starred in *Great Expectations* at Casa Mañana and the director told her she was a Texas Helena Bonham Carter. Now she plays Miss Havisham every year at our Dickens on the Square event. Plus, she's had a string of bad romances. I believe she was even stood up at the altar. I wonder if she gets that she's become the cliché she plays."

"Hell, Ses, she was on her knees, picking up pieces of glass and cradling them to her chest and she's got all these little cuts up and down her arms. I tried to help her up but she called me every obscenity in the book, so I backed off."

"Yikes!"

"And then the cops show up and there I am in flip-flops, boxer briefs, and a terry-cloth robe. Not one of my finer moments."

"I can't believe I didn't hear about this. Big doings for Twilight."

"They arrested me for trespassing and destruction of private property. Lily Munster—aka Miss Pendergarten—is hopping around saying I did it all on purpose. This morning, when I'm arraigned in front of Judge Blackthorne, I learn she had those neon lips special made in Vegas and they cost ten thousand dollars. Can you believe that?"

"Neon sculptures are expensive."

"The judge ordered me to pay for the damn lips and sentenced me to the forty hours of community service."

Sesty pressed her lips together to keep them from twitching into a sucks-to-be-you smile. "So you're a hardened criminal now. Wonder how that will play into your bio for the bachelor auction program."

He did have that bad boy aura, rough-edged and manly—his unruly hair clinging to the back of his neck, stylishly shaggy, his jaw a couple of days past a scrape with a razor, the back of his hands nicked with scars. How was it possible for him to look so devastatingly handsome? Especially to a woman who just two weeks ago was in a committed relationship.

Ah, but long before Chad there was Josh, her high school sweetheart.

"I wonder why Judge Blackthorne sent you to me?" she mused. "There's plenty of other ways for you to serve out community service. Picking up trash on the side of the road comes to mind."

"He probably thought having me work for my ex-girlfriend would be added punishment."

"Is it?" she asked. "Added punishment?"

His eyes gobbled her up. "Not from where I'm sitting."

Unnerved, she glanced away, and noticed that overhead, the toddler-sized papier-mâché Cupid was really swinging hard and fasting in the heater vent blast. Mocking her.

"This isn't the first time your impulsiveness has gotten you into trouble," she pointed out. "I remember when you and your buddies started a food fight in the high school cafeteria and you got a three day suspension."

"Yeah, my old pal Duck's fascination with *Animal House* might have had something to do with that. Duck fancied himself a young Bluto."

"And of course you fancied yourself in the Tim Mattison role. Wisest of the wise-asses."

Josh grinned, slick and naughty. Not denying it. His wicked wit and verve for life was what had once attracted her to him. He made her feel entertained, dazzled, inspired, on fire.

"Whatever happened to Duck?" she asked.

"Hate to say he followed in John Belushi's footsteps. I lost touch with him when he got into drugs. I heard he went to prison."

"I'm happy you avoided going down with him."

"We all have to grow up sometime or pay the price," Josh said. "Foolishly kidding around was how I lost you." Then in a softer voice, he murmured, "It was the biggest regret if my life."

A weight settled in the pit of her stomach. Why was he telling her this?

They stared at each other a long moment and Sesty forgot to breath. *Stop it. Remember that you swore off romantic relationships for the time being, and you swore off Josh Langtree for good.*

But he was looking at her with smoldering eyes and that I'd-love-to-see-you-naked smile that made her forget every reasonable objection against feeling this way.

She thought about Chad and her college boyfriend, Avery. How neither man could measure up to Josh. Why had they been so good in bed together? Was it Josh's skill? Or was it the way she felt when she was with him that had made the sex so freaking explosive? Maybe it was nothing more than being seventeen and in love for the first time. Maybe if they had sex now, it would be just as placid with him as it had been with Chad and Avery.

Ha! Just look at him, nothing placid about that guy.

Still, she couldn't help thinking it might be fun to give it a go. Hot sex. No strings attached. Old times' sake.

Especially since she had no idea how to do casual sex.

Yeah, but what if she slept with him and discovered too late that she simply couldn't do casual sex and he broke her heart? He was her high school sweetheart, and Twilight was known for its Sweetheart legend.

And yet, how many quarters had she tossed into the

Sweetheart Fountain, secretly hoping the legend was true? That if you tossed a coin into the fountain, you'd be reunited with your one true love.

A dozen? More? None lately, but once upon a time she'd lost a few bucks to the fountain.

"You're not the only one soured on Valentine's Day," she confessed.

His eyes narrowed and he canted his head. "You too?"

"Me."

"Miss Valentine's Day is my favorite holiday?"

She gave a wry, one-shoulder shrug. "You know how it is. Things change."

"Why? What happened?"

"Cheating, rat fink boyfriend."

"Ah, but mine was a fiancée."

"Mine happened just two weeks ago."

"She did it with my best friend."

"Okay, you win. Your heart is more broken than mine." She assessed him. Just how heartbroken over his ex was he?

"It's not a competition," he said. "Any way you slice it, getting cheated on stinks."

"Yes," she agreed.

"And yet, here you are, putting on the town's big Valentine's Day bash."

"What can I do? It's my job."

"Call in sick."

"You know I would never do that. Besides, my career hinges on making this the most successful Valentine's Day event ever."

"Doesn't mean we can't curl up our lips at love in secret whenever we're together." With his index fingers he drew the shape of a heart, then made a fist and punched the air where the imaginary heart dangled. "Down with Valentine's Day."

"Love stinks," she said, fully getting into the V-Day bashing.

"Yeah, yeah." He hummed the J. Geils Band tune.

"Hiss, boo love."

"Goopy holiday."

"Cupid should be thrown in jail. Diapered dude going around wreaking general havoc on people's lives."

"To hell with bicycles built for two."

"All this fuss over phenethylamine," she exclaimed.

"What's that?" he asked.

"The love chemical. It's in chocolate. Why do you think they sell more chocolate during Valentine's Day than any other time of the year?"

"Capitalist bastards. Taking advantage of hapless humans held hostage by hormones."

"It's not *really* love, just a chemical reaction in your brain."

"A case of temporary insanity."

"I've never felt so close to you," she teased.

"Solidarity in the Valentine's Haters Club." He held up a palm and she slapped him a high five.

The waitress reappeared to clear their plates. "Dessert?"

Josh wiggled his eyebrows. "I think we deserve something decadent to help us mend our broken hearts, don't you?" he said to Sesty.

She was about to slide her cell phone from her purse to check the time, but stopped herself. He was right. She did overschedule her entire life. "What the heck? Want to split something?"

"Sure," he said. "But in a totally nonromantic way."

"Of course. None of that syrupy mess going on around here."

"What's your most popular dessert?" Josh asked the waitress.

"Ever since Rinky-Tink's went out of business," the waitress said, referring to a formerly favorite ice cream store on the town square, "our top seller has been the ice cream sundae."

"Bring us one of those." He held up two fingers. "Couple of spoons."

"On it." The waitress left.

Josh turned back to Sesty. "Hot fudge sundae okay with you?"

"It's a little late to ask my opinion."

"Sorry, that was rude of me. And it's chocolate. Do we want to risk it with that phenethylamine stuff? Should I catch her and change our order?"

"I'm just yanking your chain. I love hot fudge sundaes, and if I hadn't, I would have spoken up. I'm not that simpering girl you used to know."

"You were never simpering."

"I used to be much more of a people pleaser."

"What changed?" he asked.

"Breaking up with you. I kept thinking if I'd spoken up sooner, maybe things wouldn't have come to a head the way they did. Then again, I was dating Chad because my friends and family liked him, and look what happened."

"Chad?"

"The cheating rat fink boyfriend."

When the waitress returned, she set a massive hot fudge sundae in the middle of the table. After she left, they both stared at the chocolate oozing down the ice cream, then looked up at each other.

"Do we roll the dice?" he whispered.

"I think we're safe."

"How's that?"

"You build up a tolerance to phenethylamine over time," she said, "and then it eventually stops working."

"So because you and I have been down this road together before, phenethylamine can't suck us into something we don't want to get sucked into?"

"I'm no scientist. I only know this stuff about phenethylamine because I researched it while planning the bachelor auction. I'm passing out chocolate candy at the door. Get those women in the mood to bid high."

"Wow." He looked impressed. "You do throw yourself into your work."

"And you don't, Mr. Hard Driver?"

"How did you know that's the excuse Miley gave me as the reason she slept with Dave?"

"Miley the ex?"

He nodded. "She said I spent too much time under the hood of a car instead of under her."

"She favored the woman-on-top position?"

"She favored the Miley-on-top-of-my-best-friend position."

"You deserve better," she said, and truly meant it.

Josh's laugh was sardonic. "Aren't we a pair? Both of us duped and dumped."

"No one to hold hands with on Valentine's Day and send sappy cards to and—"

"We dodged a bullet," Josh said. "At least to my way of thinking."

"Did we? Two Valentine's haters stuck working a bachelor auction together. Sounds kinda pathetic if you ask me."

"It could be worse."

"How's that?"

"We could be falling for the mushy hype like those two over there." He nodded toward a lovey-dovey couple in a corner booth. They were sitting on the same side of the table cozying up and feeding each other bites from their plates.

"Eye rolling," she said.

"Get out the Pepto."

"Why don't they just book a room?"

"Call a doctor. Looks to me like phenethylamine overdose."

"Oooh darling." She clasped her hands together, tucked her pressed palms against her left cheek and fluttered her eyelashes at him. "Give me another bite. I'm too helplessly in love with you to lift my own spoon."

"Here you go, sweetums." He dipped his spoon into the sundae, served up a morsel of vanilla ice cream dripping with hot fudge, chopped nuts, and whipped cream to her lips. "I love it when you lick my spoon clean."

"Mmm." She opened her mouth and he slipped the cold spoonful of ice cream over her tongue.

It was a shock. The cold. The fact he was feeding her. The realization that she was letting him.

She swallowed quickly. Too quickly. Her throat seized up.

"Ses? You okay?" Josh leaned forward, put his hand on top of hers.

That didn't help. Not one bit. She shook her head, put her palm to the throat.

"Are you choking?"

"No." She panted. "Killer brain freeze."

That's when a loud creaking noise from overhead drew their attention upward, just as Cupid broke from the chain anchoring him to the ceiling and came tumbling down on top of them.

Chapter Four

AFTER THEY PICKED the plaster from their hair following Cupid's revenge at Pappa Pasta's, Josh and Sesty went to the small office she rented above an art gallery on the town square. She unlocked the door and entered ahead of Josh. He couldn't resist staring at her butt. How many times had he cupped that sweet bumper in his palm?

Your loss buddy. You let her get away.

And for what? The adrenaline thrill of NASCAR?

Hell yeah, he did love the sport, but now that he'd been sidelined, he was starting to understand just how narrow and stunted his life had become. He could drive a car fast and that was about it. Where Sesty had grown and changed, he'd become stagnant, zooming endlessly around track after track. No wonder Miley had gone looking for love in other places. He'd become completely self-absorbed.

Hollow. He felt a hollowness deep in his belly. He

shook his head. This self-examination crap was for the birds.

"Ta-da." Sesty spun in a small circle, arms outstretched.

The room was long and narrow, and if her arms were a foot longer, she could have touched both walls. The entire town square of Twilight was listed in the historic registry, and proudly carried the mark of its pioneer heritage. In keeping with the theme, an antique rolltop desk sat in the corner, stacked neatly with piles of paper and color-coded folders, and there were old black and white framed photos on the wall of the town back in the late 1800s.

Sesty's eyes glistened like a hand-polished hood in the noonday sun. "My own office space."

"The inner sanctum."

"As long as I can afford it." She nibbled her bottom lip.

Josh couldn't help wishing he were the one snacking on that sweet pink mouth. "Money woes?"

"Always. That's why doing a good job with this bachelor auction means so much to me. If I can't get legs under my event planning business . . ."

"It's back to the B&B?"

She nodded.

"Would that be so bad? You used to love working there."

"It's not that I don't like working at the B&B." She hesitated, jiggling her foot back and forth against the creaky wooden flooring of the old building. "It's that I need to find my own place in the world. Make a mark that's separate from my parents."

"Breathing room from Jim and Marcie. I get that."

The office door opened and Jana came bopping inside, but stopped in midstride when she spotted him. "What are you doing here? Not that I mind. In fact . . ." Jana sent an approving gaze over his body. "I don't mind at all."

"Slave labor." Josh winked.

Jana boldly winked back. "So what are you guys up to? Need any help?"

"We're making the set designs," Sesty said. "Sawing and sanding and painting. With your asthma, you might want to avoid the office of the rest of the day."

"Thanks for the heads-up. I have a situation I need to handle anyway."

"What's up?"

"The stage manager called. We've run afoul of some stagehand union rules that will impact the budget for the auction. I'm going over there to see if I can't smooth things over." Jana unbuttoned two buttons on her blouse, revealing an abundance of cleavage.

"Jana!" Sesty exclaimed.

"What?" Jana grinned. "The stage manager's got a crush on me. I'd be dumb not to use that in negotiations.

"Please do up at least one button."

"Okay. For you." Jana sent her a tolerant smile and buttoned one of the buttons she'd just undone. "I'll send you a text to let you know how it goes."

She left with an over-the-shoulder wave.

"She's just going to unbutton it again when she gets outside," Josh predicted.

"I know."

"She's not the kind of partner I would have pictured you with."

"I know that too. But I like Jana. She pushes me out of my comfort zone." Sesty slipped out of his jacket and handed it to him. "Let's get down to work."

Her soft fragrance rose up from his jacket, sweet and flowery. God, she smelled good. He had a driving impulse to bury his nose in her hair and take a long deep whiff. Over the years, whenever he thought of Twilight, this was the scent that came to him—honest, clean, homey. Unnerved and suddenly way too warm himself, he draped the jacket over a high-backed chair and cleared his throat.

She went to the closet, flung it open and started dragging out three large plywood planks.

"Hey, hey, let me do that," he said, high-stepping over to wrestle the plywood from her hands. His knee twinged a warning. *Watch it.*

"I can do it," she insisted.

"I didn't say you couldn't."

"So let me do it."

"While I admire this independent streak of yours, I'm the man, and I'll be doing the heavy lifting," he insisted. "Isn't that why I'm here in the first place?"

"Actually, you're here because you busted Miss Pendergarten's lips."

"True that." He loved the saucy look on her. She should tease more. "But when you put it like that, my crime sounds dastardly."

"My mother always said you were on the road to ruin."

Her smile, tender with amusement, crinkled her eyes and his heart.

"So did mine." He chuckled.

They stared at each other, three sheets of plywood between them. Good thing too, otherwise he just might have kissed her, and that would have been really stupid. They both were on the rebound, and even if they weren't, there was too much history here.

Sesty was the first to look away. "We should get to work."

"Yeah," he croaked. He wished he came equipped with a bleeder valve so he could release some of the sexual pressure building inside him. "What are we doing exactly?"

"Constructing the sets for the bachelor auction. Here are the plans." She handed him blueprints of the set designs. "Are you good with your hands?"

"Is your memory that faulty?" he couldn't resist asking.

Her cheeks flamed red, but she didn't say anything else, just reached into the closet for a leather tool belt and extended it toward him.

He hesitated. Eyed the belt. "Did this belong to Chad?"

"No," she said. "It's mine. Chad was useless with tools."

Josh bit down on his tongue to keep from saying, *Lucky for me.* He might as well fall to his knees and beg for trouble. Damn, he wanted her. How did a man stop himself from wanting a woman he shouldn't want?

You managed it ten years ago. How'd you do it then?

Oh, yeah, she'd kicked him out of her life for his reckless behavior. But that "recklessness" had led him to his career, and that career was what kept his mind off losing her.

A career that had lost its shine.

His knee twinged again, dark thoughts for another time. He slapped a grin on his face, readjusted the tool belt to fit, and strapped it on.

Sesty studied him, head canted, lips pursed, and unless he missed his guess, he saw a hot flare of interest in her dark blue eyes. Some women got charged up over men in tool belts. Did she?

Just in case she did, he positioned the belt low on his hips like a cowboy's holster. Her gaze tracked his every move. Yep. He definitely had her attention.

"I'll need a saw," he said.

"Got one." She reached into the closet for a jigsaw.

"Should have known." He moved to take the saw from her. "Some things never change. You always were prepared."

"Not on the night that—" She broke off, shook her head. "Never mind that."

Yeah, he didn't want to talk about that night either. The night she broke up with him in the police station after their parents came to pick them up, following their spectacular crash into the Sweetheart Fountain.

It was the first time he'd had his heart ripped from his chest and torn to shreds. He thought of the old Rod Stewart song, "First Cut is the Deepest," and turned away from her with the saw tucked tight against his chest.

Forty hours.

Just get through the forty hours with her. If he could

survive working so close to her for forty hours, he could survive any test of will and come out unbreakable.

HER TINY OFFICE was not the best place to do sawing and hammering and painting, but she really had nowhere else for them to work besides her own home, and she wasn't about to take him there. The setting was too intimate, too ripe for temptation.

Gad! You have to stop thinking like this. There is nothing between you and Josh.

That ship had sailed a long time ago. Yes, he was sexier than ever. Yes, every time she looked at him, her body heated up in troublesome places. And yes, she kept imagining doing the most scandalous things with and to him. But she'd been scorched by love, and he'd been the first one to set her ablaze. How stupid would she be to go back for third degree burns?

They worked for hours on the set pieces. She held the plywood in place over two saw horses while he cut out the designs—a box of chocolates, a teddy bear wearing a heart-shaped bow, Cupid, again, slinging an arrow. Sawdust flew. Goggles protected their eyes, but sawdust got in their hair, clung to their clothes, landed on their lips.

Once the cutting was done they took a break and swept up the mess. Sesty pulled two bottles of water from the minifridge in the corner and passed one to him.

"Thanks." Josh ran the back of his arm over his forehead, which was beaded with manly perspiration, and then tilted back his head and took a long drink.

Sesty's gaze hung on the column of his throat and watched his powerful neck muscles gulp down the water. She remembered what it felt like to run her palms over his bare chest, finger the taut ripples of his hard planes and lines. Instantly, her body reacted. Tingling, tightening, moistening.

To distract herself, she moved to the closet, found the sandpaper and hand sander she'd gotten from her father, put her goggles back on and started sanding the teddy bear cutout.

"Do you have another sander?" he asked, coming over to squat down beside her.

"Only the one."

"Then let me do the sanding."

"I've got it." She bumped his shoulder with hers, muscling him out of her personal space.

"You sure hate giving up control."

"No more so than you."

"I'm no control freak," he denied.

"The heck you aren't. I've heard people talking. They say the reason you wrecked during your last race was because you thought you knew better than your crew chief."

"Yeah, well, it's easy for people to be armchair pit crew. They have absolutely no idea what it's really like out there on the track." He got a faraway look in his eyes.

"What *is* it like?" she prodded.

"Scary, exhilarating, a complete physical and mental rush. Actually, it's a whole lot like great sex." His gaze lingered on her breasts.

She ignored that last part. "How difficult is it?"

"It requires one hundred percent concentration. One wrong move and poof!" He clapped his hands, flinging fine particles of sawdust into the air. "It's all over."

Which was precisely why she'd broken up with him. She couldn't handle loving a daredevil, knowing that at any moment one wrong turn and he'd never come home to her.

"Is it true? Did you crash because you didn't listen to your crew chief?"

"It's true that I don't like to be controlled."

"Who does? Now do you understand why I want to wield my own sander?"

Josh flapped a permissive hand. "Okay. You've made your point. Sand away."

"Thank you for getting out of my way." She pushed her goggles back down over her face and went back to the sanding, pressing her lips into a straight light, keeping her attention fully focused on the task at hand. Taking no notice, as best she could, of the masculine man sitting on the floor beside her.

The vibrating sander sent tremors up her palm, through her arm, and into her shoulder. The sander hit a rough patch on the plywood, made a revving noise.

She switched it off and raised her goggles for a closer look. There was a divot where the jigsaw blade had hung in the plywood, cutting a small chunk from the side of the teddy bear's face.

"Oh no," she exclaimed.

"What is it?"

"Teddy's ruined."

"What do you mean?"

"Look here." She traced an index finger over the flaw.

"What?"

"The cut is jagged."

"So?"

"We need to cut out a new teddy Bear. I've bought a couple of extra pieces of plywood just in case something like this happened."

"Excuse me?" He cupped his palm around an ear.

"We've got to cut out a new—"

"I heard what you said, but I can't believe my ears. You're going to throw out this cutout because of one little mistake?"

"It's on the bear's face where everyone can see."

"Big deal. This is a set design that will be used once. People aren't going to be inspecting it with a magnifying glass. Odds are no one will notice."

"*I'll* know."

"Sesty, you've got to be joking."

"Don't you see how important this is? The event has to go off without a hitch. If I screw this up, I've lost my shot."

"You're not going to screw it up."

"I will if I let subpar work go up on that stage." She prodded the divot with her finger and more wood fell out.

"Stop poking at it!"

"I can't. Do you think I'm OCD?"

"Ses." He laid a firm hand on her shoulder and gently tilted her around to face him. "Trust me. It's going to be okay. Everyone will be looking at the bachelors anyway. Let it go."

She cast a glance over her shoulder. The light caught the cutout just right, making the irregular cut look like a deep gash. Yes, she was being irrational and she knew it, but knowledge couldn't counter the anxiety punching her stomach. "It's not perfect."

He took her chin between his fingers and thumb and forcefully turned her head back to meet his gaze.

She averted his eyes. His stare was simply too intense.

"Look at me."

Reluctantly, she met his eyes. Dark pools of chocolate, warm and inviting, enticed her to jump right in.

"Do you know anyone who is perfect?" he asked.

"No," she admitted. She didn't know why the flawed cutout bothered her so much, but it did.

"You sure about that?" He lowered his head.

"Yes." She felt kind of silly now. "Nobody's perfect."

"Then why do you feel like *you* have to be perfect all the time? It's a losing battle. Why do you do that to yourself?"

It was a good question, a rational question. Too bad she didn't have a rational answer.

"Because," she explained, as the stomach anxiety pole-vaulted into her throat, "if I'm not perfect, I won't be good enough."

"Good enough for what?"

And without even knowing she was thinking it, Sesty blurted, "To be loved."

He peered at her for a long moment. "Honey, anyone who would reject you because you have flaws isn't worthy of *your* love. You're lovable just the way you are—an imperfect perfectionist, who tries her best to please everyone but herself."

"You think I'm lovable?" She breathed, unable to believe she was asking him. It was pathetic. A competent woman didn't go fishing for compliments. She earned them.

"Smart, gorgeous, obsessive, insecure, what's not to love?" He laughed.

"Those last two don't sound like lovable qualities to me."

"Are you kidding me?" He smiled kindly—much more than kindly—it was a smile brimming with encouragement and belief. In her. A tingle went up and down her spine, sparkly and hot. "Those last two qualities are what make you the most lovable."

"How's that?"

"If you were truly perfect, everyone would hate your guts."

"But I'll never be perfect."

"Bull's-eye."

"So I should just stop striving for excellence?"

"Not excellence, perfection."

"I don't know the difference."

His smile flipped over. "Redoing the cutout means that much to you, huh?"

"Yes."

He put out his hand. "Give me that jigsaw.

This was silliness. They didn't have time to redo the cutout. Why was she being so picky?

A memory washed over her. Something she'd tucked

away in the back of her brain and shut the door on, but it returned to her now with startling clarity. She was nine years old and struggling in math and her usual straight A's had taken a hit. She'd gotten a C. Knees shaking, palms sweating, stomach aching, she approached her parents with the wretched report card to sign.

Her mother had taken the report card from her, scowled darkly. "What is this, young lady?"

"A C!" her father exploded. "Snows do not make C's!"

She burst into tears, apologized profusely for her failings. It hadn't mattered. Her parents scolded her. "You've let us down. We are so disappointed in you." That night they did not tuck her in bed as they did every other night. "We can't look at you right now," her father said when he sent her to her room without dinner as her punishment.

Left alone in the dark, sobbing into a pillow, she had made a vow. She would always strive to be perfect. If she were perfect, her parents would not be disappointed in her.

Throughout her life she had received that same message loud and clear, from her parents, from teachers, from Chad, from society at large. *The world values champions.* Therefore, in order to be loved, she could not fail.

The only person who had not expected perfection from her, had in fact encouraged her to fail and fail spectacularly, was Josh.

"Hey," he'd said to her once. "If I didn't wreck cars, I wouldn't learn how to drive skillfully. You've got to crash a few times in order to get better. You never crash, you never succeed."

Of course, that was why she'd broken up with him—over a crash, over a flaw. The night they totaled her parents' car, smashing through the park and into the Sweetheart Fountain, Josh hadn't been behind the wheel.

She had.

But he'd been the one to take the blame. Before the police had gotten there, he made her switch seats with him. In the end, her parents vilified Josh, and she felt she had no choice but to pick them over him.

And now here he was, doing it all over again. Pushing her to accept her flaws as a lovable part of who she was.

It felt wonderfully strange.

Chapter Five

TEN P.M. WAS late for Twilight, and the streets stretched empty when they emerged from her office after cutting, sanding, and painting perfect set designs for the bachelor auction. While they'd been inside, city workers had twined red, white, and pink twinkle lights throughout the trees on the courthouse lawn and in nearby Sweetheart Park.

"Well." Sesty paused on the street outside the art gallery featuring kitschy, Texas objects d'art. "This is goodnight."

Josh didn't make a move.

Neither did she.

They stood peering into each other's eyes, surrounded by the smell of sawdust, acrylic paint, and the night breeze wafting off Lake Twilight, but in spite of the cool temperature, she wasn't cold.

"I'll walk you to your car," he said.

"No need," she replied breathlessly. "I don't require a bodyguard. Remember, you're back in Twilight. Not some big city."

"I'm walking you to your car," he insisted. "And I'm not taking no for an answer. Where are you parked?"

"I'm not. I walked. I have a house over on Prosper Lane."

"That's a half a mile away. You definitely are not walking home in the dark."

"All right," she said. Twilight was a safe place, but sometimes, in the dark, the mind could play tricks with shadows, and she welcomed his company.

"Let's cut through the park," he said, and put a proprietary hand to the small of her back.

"There's a curfew in effect for the park." She was so aware of his hand, but didn't try to shake him loose. "It closes at ten."

"Since when?"

"There was some trouble a few years back with teenagers hanging out in the park after hours, drinking and making mischief."

"It's only a few minutes after ten. And how do you close a park anyway?"

"The cops patrol through here pretty frequently."

"If they catch us, we'll just explain we're cutting through, not loitering. We're both well over twenty-one."

She swatted at him, felt giggly and girly. "Oh, you and your bad boy ways."

"C'mon." He winked. "Live a little."

How many times had he said that to her in the past? Too many to count.

"What's the worst that could happen if we get caught?" he whispered, lowering his head close to her ear. "They call our parents?"

Silly as it was, that gave her pause. What would her parents say if they heard she'd gotten caught trespassing in Sweetheart Park after hours with Josh Langtree? She shook off the impulse. It was past time she stopped caring about what her parents thought. She loved them, but she'd allowed them to dominate her life for too long. Their approval of Chad had been one of the reasons she started dating him in the first place, and look where that road had taken her—to a big fat dead end.

The light pressure of his palm against her spine triggered something inside her. A click. A pop. A settling into place, like the pieces of a puzzle coming together to form a cohesive whole.

Feels like old times.

He guided her over the wooden bridge that spanned a fingerling tributary of the Brazos River. They'd traversed this path many times before. Usually, holding hands or with their palms tucked in each other's back pockets. Nostalgia made her smile at the girl she'd once been.

Hard plastic Valentine's Day ornaments had been hung from the trees and they shone brightly in the reflection of the colorful twinkle lights. Hearts. Flowers. Cupids. Cheesy, yes but it was a little romantic too, she had to admit.

"They rope you in with it, don't they?" Josh said, as if reading her thoughts. "No matter how hard you try to resist Valentine's Day mania, you can't escape it in this town."

"From a purely practical standpoint, it's all about pulling tourism dollars into our town. It's Twilight's lifeblood, after all."

"All the hype makes it hard not to succumb to the illusion, but I'm not falling for the hokum." Josh's staunch jaw tightened.

"Me either."

"Seems like we're the only sane people in town when it comes being immune to Valentine's Day."

"Seems like," she murmured, but a wisp of sadness tugged at her heart. She liked the sweet fantasy of one true love, but it was just that, wasn't it? A fantasy and nothing more.

They left the wooden footbridge, strolled down the paved path that skirted the water's edge. His hand was still at her back. She was so aware of it. Of him.

It had been ten years since she'd seen him, but it seemed no longer than a heartbeat. Was it really possible? To pick up the threads of a tattered relationship, only to find they'd never broken? She tried to breathe, but hope tangled up in her lungs, twisted around until she thought she might suffocate on the feeling.

Inhale. Exhale. Inhale.

Up ahead lay the Sweetheart Tree, crowned with a red lights entwined around a heart-shaped wire frame. Josh stopped in front of it, a come-be-bad-with-me smile plucking at his lips as he studied the trunk of the old pecan.

"The Sweetheart Tree is still here." He sounded amazed.

"It's been here for over a century. Why wouldn't it be?"

"How long do pecans live, for godsakes?"

"Apparently more than a hundred years."

"Even with all the carvings."

"We never carved our name into the tree like everyone else did," she said.

"Because you wouldn't let me."

"The sign says not to. It's bad for the tree."

"And you always follow the rules when no one else does." His voice was weighted, with both amusement and exasperation.

"And you were dead set on breaking all of them." When she was in high school, she'd primly told him that the rules were there for a reason, but now a bittersweet melancholia settled over her. She wished she *had* let him carve their names in the tree.

He dropped his hand and stepped to the south side of the tree, settled his arms on his hips, stared at the names carved there of all the couples who'd been in love. Jesse and Flynn. Sam and Emma. Travis and Sarah. Caitlyn and Gideon. It was a virtual who's who of local lovers.

Intrigued, she moved to stand beside him. "What are you looking for?"

His mouth twitched but he didn't look at her. He was busy with his search.

Suspicion sneaked up on her. "Did you carve our name

in the tree after I asked you not to?" Part of her was thrilled at the idea that he might have gone to all the trouble, while the good girl part of her was appalled to think he'd marred the tree.

He didn't answer, but took car keys from his pocket. There was a tiny flashlight on the key chain. He turned in on, flashed the light over the bark. "Ah," he said. "Here it is."

"I should have known you couldn't resist breaking the rules." She inched closer, her body brushing up against his back as she peered up to where he was shining the light. "Where is it? I don't see our names carved there."

"Keep looking."

She squinted, reached out a finger to trace the names, *Jon loves Rebekka*, the original sweethearts who were part of the town founders, and the first to carve their names into the tree.

Sesty found other names. People she knew well. Rule breakers. Tree defacers. All in the name of love. Now, because Josh had carved her name there, she was one of those rule-breakers too. Why did that feel so exciting?

"I'm sorry, but I still don't see it."

"It's right under your nose, Ses."

Huh? No matter how she searched, she did not see their names carved into the tree. Wait a minute. What was that?

There, in a flat bark-free area of the tree, just above Jon's declaration of love for Rebekka, she spied faded red nail polish. The lacquered lettering was thin and patches of it had flaked off, so she could just barely make it out. *Josh loves Sesty.*

Loves.

Oh my. She put a palm to her mouth and a hard knot bloomed in the dead center of her chest.

"I didn't carve it," he said. "I promised you I wouldn't carve our names in the tree, so I stole a bottle of my sister's nail polish and I painted it there instead."

"The years have almost worn it away." She couldn't seem to catch her breath, her fingers still tracing the lettering.

"But not quite."

"We were so silly then. Thinking our puppy love would last forever."

"Nothing lasts forever." He sounded glib.

Typical Josh. Nothing got to him. Everything rolled right off his back, but when she looked up, she saw a what-might-have-happened-if-I'd-chosen-a-different-path expression on his face. The longing and regret in his eyes matched the tightening of her throat. Could he see it on her too?

Thrown off guard, she ducked her head, stepped back. "I better be getting home. Tomorrow is a busy day."

"Zesty Sesty," he whispered.

He was standing above her, one hand resting on the bark of the Sweetheart Tree; his head tilted downward, his eyes twinkling from the blink of Valentine lights. On his face was an expression of raw, honest sexual hunger.

He wanted her.

Sesty gulped. She wanted him too.

Oh no, no, no. You're on the rebound. Josh is water under the bridge. He's—

But that's as far as she got in her mental argument.

He hooked two fingers underneath her chin, lifted her face up to his, lowered his head and kissed her.

She did not resist. In fact, if she were being quite honest, she met him halfway. Although she wasn't really ready to admit that to herself, but her arms slipped around his neck as his mouth branded hers. She inhaled the rich taste of him, parted her lips.

Sweet Lord, but he tasted sensational.

A banquet after a starvation diet wouldn't have tasted this good. She had to have more. Greedy, greedy. Surely it was a sin to feel this greedy.

His tongue touched hers, hot and searching.

Sesty sagged against him. He wrapped his arms around her, pulling her closer. It had been so long since she'd felt the hard planes of his body against her curves, but it was a sensation she'd never forgotten. Her first time had been with this man. She'd given him her virginity without regret and she would always remember him, no matter where she ended up or whom she eventually married or how old she got.

Josh was her first. There could be no changing that. She didn't want to change it.

Don't get swept away on emotions. You know how fickle feelings can be. You loved him once and mourned the loss of him for way longer than you should have. Do you really want to get back on that ride?

Yeah, the argument sounded good in theory, but she wasn't listening. All she could hear was the steady pounding of their hearts beating in perfect harmony.

The kiss grew deeper, slower, a quiet inner pool amid the hard pull of sexual current flowing between them. His masterful tongue teased, drawing responses from her body that she never thought possible. She felt as if she were leaping off the old suspension bridge they used to dive off into the Brazos River back when they were in high school. Hitting the surface with a shocking smack of impact, falling into the languid arms of the water.

She threaded her fingers through his hair, tugged lightly, holding him in place. The world shrank to the width if their mouths. She knew every part of him. Had been here before, and while it felt hauntingly familiar, there was the spicy undertones of a stranger.

Ten years lay between. They'd both changed. Grown. Had experiences without each other. The sensation was novel, disconcerting, surprising, and oddly comfortable. How could a man be both known and mysterious?

He increased the pressure. Their bodies were molded to each other. His rock hard, hers moist and pliant. He made her feel sexy and wanted and accepted and needed and valued. It was a heady experience, and she had to ask herself some hard questions.

Was this merely a blast from the past? A melancholy trip down memory lane? Or was she secretly hoping for more and setting herself up for heartache?

But in the throes of passion, she could not answer such weighted questions. She gave herself into the moment, fully experiencing everything it had to offer. Requiring nothing from this space in time except to enjoy herself.

Finally, Josh pulled away from her, leaving her raw and achy and wanting more.

Dammit, she should have been the first one to pull away. She stepped back, straightened, and combed her fingers through her hair. Tried to look cool and completely unruffled.

His breathing was ragged, more ragged than hers. Good. She wasn't the only one who'd been thrown for a loop.

He cupped her cheek with his palm, stared deeply into her eyes. "We're in trouble here."

"Not really," she denied glibly. "It was just a kiss. We've kissed before."

"This one was different."

"Only because we're older, more experienced. It's not—"

He kissed her again, sucking her into his orbit. Was this how all his fan girls felt?

She splayed a palm against his chest, pushed back. "You gotta stop doing that."

"Why?"

"We hate all things romantic, remember?"

"This doesn't have to be the least bit romantic, Ses."

"Hmm, I fear we're a little too late for that. Walking in the park, finding where you painted our names on the Sweetheart Tree. This is bordering on so damn sweet it could rot our teeth."

"If you think this is sweet, then I've been doing it wrong," he said.

And by damn, he kissed her again and there was nothing sweet about it.

A moan slipped from her lips and escaped into the cold night air. His body heat scalded her, invaded her, as relentless as that amazing tongue. He opened his mouth wider around hers, drank her up.

This was going to end up someplace they could very well live to regret. If she didn't want Valentine's Day to be forever connected to this night, she needed to put a stop to this.

Right now.

But she simply could not bring herself to let go of him. It felt too good. Maybe she could do casual sex. Why not?

Because this is Josh we're talking about.

His hands slipped up underneath her coat, his palms sliding up her back. Big hands. Capable hands. Hands that gripped a steering wheel and kept expensive cars on a track at two hundred miles an hour.

Just one more taste and she'd hit the brakes.

His body grew harder, letting her know exactly how much he wanted her. How was it possible for a man to be so hard? Scary, his arousal. But exciting too. Her self-esteem had taken a battering from Chad's betrayal, but Josh's desire made her feel powerful. Not only that, but she longed to prove Chad wrong. That she *was* good in bed. At least with Josh.

He nuzzled her neck. Dear God, he smelled so good. Masculine. Woodsy. His mouth claimed hers once more. One hand pushed up the back of her neck, his fingers spearing through her hair. The other wrapped tightly around her waist as if he would never let her go.

Without even realizing it, she'd been dreaming of a moment like this ever since they'd broken up. A sweet reunion. Reunited. All misunderstandings cleared up. Everything forgiven.

You're romanticizing this. You're wounded. He's wounded. You're taking solace from each other, nothing more. If this was meant to be, do you think it really would have taken him ten years to show up?

Yeah, yeah, she knew that, but old fantasies died hard.

Except this reality was even better than those she'd dreamed. He was so hot and welcoming, comforting as a fire in the fireplace on a stormy winter night. Her high school sweetheart was in her arms once more.

"Do you . . ." She gathered her courage and stared straight into his eyes. ". . . want to come home with me?"

Before he could answer, headlights cut through the night, spotlighting them.

The car stopped on the road beside the park.

A siren gave a short blast. Blue and red lights flashed.

Oh, crap. It was the cops.

Chapter Six

THE NEXT MORNING, Jana arrived at the office the same
time as Sesty. Her assistant carried a backpack over her
left shoulder, her tablet computer in one hand and an
extra tall cup of coffee from Perks in the other.

Sesty eyed the cup longingly. Why did coffee made at
a coffee shop taste better than what she brewed at home?

"Somebody was busy last night," Jana said in a sing-
song voice.

"Yes." Sesty glanced around at the cutouts she and
Josh had stacked around the office last night to dry. "We
completed all the set designs. Another item we tick off
our to-do list."

"That's not what I'm talking about." The look in Jana's
maverick eyes told Sesty something was up and her assistant approved of it. "I heard you got a ticket for kissing
Josh Langtree in the park."

She bit back a groan. "I didn't get a—"

"Hey, don't be ashamed. Chad hasn't put a ring on it or anything." Jana shot a spiky glance at the third finger of Sesty's left hand. "A girl has needs, and if Chad's not meeting them . . ."

"We broke up."

"What?"

"Chad and I broke up."

"When? Why didn't you tell me?"

"Two weeks ago. Chad dumped me for the new barista at Perks."

"Skank!"

"Chad or the barista or me?"

"Certainly not you."

"I *was* kissing Josh in the park."

"Good for you."

"Does that make me a skank?"

Jana plunked her backpack down on the rolltop desk. "You worry too much about what other people think of you."

Sesty made a pretzel of her arms and laid them across her chest. "I don't feel good about it."

"What?"

"The kissing thing."

"Why not?" Jana wrinkled her nose. "Is Langtree a terrible kisser?"

"No. He's a great kisser. Maybe the best kisser ever."

"So what's the problem?"

"He was my first love."

"Ah-ha." Jana raised a finger like Sherlock Holmes

ferreting out a clue. "You're afraid of falling in love with him all over again."

"We do live in Twilight with that stupid legend that if you throw a coin into the fountain and wish for your one true love, you'll be reunited."

"Did you do it?"

"No! I did not have sex with him."

"Not that, although, why not? Did you ever throw a coin into the fountain and wish to be reunited with him?"

"Fifth amendment."

Jane took a sip from her coffee. "You are so screwed."

"Come on, that legend isn't real."

"Hey, you're the one who threw the coin into the fountain, not me."

"I'm such an idiot." Sesty pounded her forehead with the heel of her palm. "It could never work between us."

"Why not?" Jana asked reasonably.

"He is who he is."

"And who is he?"

"A NASCAR star."

"What's wrong with that?"

Sesty shrugged. "You know."

"Oh no, I'm not letting you get away with this. You are *not* claiming he's out of your league, because he's not. He would be damn lucky to have you." Jana bobbed her head so fiercely her dreadlocks shook.

"Thanks for the loyalty, but I'm talking about his career. Josh takes risks for a living—"

"And you're seriously risk averse."

Sesty pressed three fingers to her lips, took a deep breath. "It's why we split up in the first place."

"So stop kissing him."

"I don't think I can."

"Sure you can. It's called self-control, and you've got more than a monk in a monastery."

Sesty paced her way around the room, skirting the new teddy bear cutout with his pristine face. "I can't get involved with Josh."

Jana plunked down in the desk chair and watched her like she was the lead actress in a telenovela. "So don't."

"My home is here. His life is on the road. It would never work out."

"Who are you trying to convince? Me or you?"

"It's just Valentine's Day fever. I'm falling under the spell of the hype."

Jana's dreadlocks trembled again "Easy enough to do around this place."

"It's ridiculous. Just say no, right?"

"Unless you want to say yes."

"I don't . . . want to say yes."

"Then don't."

"I'm lying, I do."

"Then go to it."

"Aren't you going to give me any useful advice?"

Jana pantomimed kicking Sesty's butt. "Quit obsessing about him and get back to work."

"Thank you. I needed that."

"You're welcome. I fully expect you to kick my ass if I ever fall for this sop."

"Will do." Sesty straightened, dusted off her hands. "Did you get the issues straightened out with the stage manager?"

Jana pressed her lips together as if suppressing a smile and her eyes lit up. "It's handled. No budget increase needed."

"The cleavage worked, huh?"

"That and my natural charm." She fluttered her eyelashes. "I convinced him to get creative and find a way around the union rules."

"You are my hero," Sesty said. "What's on the agenda for today?"

Jana consulted her tablet computer. "We need to select the music that will be playing for each bachelor as he steps onto the auction block. I've already got a few suggestions." She passed the list she'd made on the tablet to Sesty. "Ain't No Other Man," "Wild Thing," "Hot Stuff," and "Burning Love."

"Ugh." Sesty sighed. "More romantic stuff we have to wade through."

"What doesn't kill us makes us stronger."

"After this event is over, I'm going to be bulletproof. Teflon. Love will bounce right off me."

"That's the spirit."

"Is it hot in here or just me?" Sesty slipped off her jacket, moved to open the window.

"Weatherman says it's supposed to be freakishly hot today. Seventy degrees or something weird, and humid to boot."

"In February?"

"Crazy, I know."

"That's good I guess, if the warmth holds out. People

will be more likely to show up for the auction if it's not cold. What does Saturday's weather forecast look like?" Sesty tapped her chin.

Jane pulled a face that looked as if she'd bitten down on aluminum foil. "You're going to hate this."

"Rain?"

"Into each life some rain must fall. Although I think the exact words the weatherman used were 'winter thunderstorm.'"

"Seriously?" *Don't whine. You're not a whiner.* "Okay, it's not a big deal. All the more reason for people to come in out of the weather and ogle our bachelors, right?"

"There you go. That's the spirit. The old Sesty is back. Looks like Josh's lips gave you the attitude adjustment you needed." Jana pumped a fist. "Rock on, Josh."

She didn't have the heart to tell her assistant her new attitude was just a big dose of fake it till you make it.

"Hey," Jana said, her voice dry but her eyes full of mirth. "I think I have the prefect song for you to play when Josh gets up to strut his stuff on stage."

Sesty fell for it. "What's that?"

"Prince. 'Kiss.'" She belted out an off-key rendition. "Perfect lyrics, iTunes here I come."

"You're enjoying my misery aren't you?"

Jana laughed with wicked glee. "Immensely."

SESTY SPENT THE rest of Thursday morning dealing with the logistics of the bachelor auction—touching base with the auctioneer, proofreading the programs before Jana sent them to the printer, meeting with the organizers of Holly's House to give them an update.

No grass grew under Jana's feet. She hustled social media with a buildup campaign that was now showcasing Josh as the premier bachelor on the auction block, and she was getting an encouraging number of retweets and Facebook likes on Twilight's Web site.

Meanwhile, Sesty was so busy that she almost forgot about Josh.

Almost, but not quite.

Just when she was completely absorbed in her work, he'd steal into her mind and rob a few minutes of her thoughts. In response, she'd snort, shove her bangs off her forehead—brush that man right out of her hair—and get back to it.

A little after one o'clock she glanced up from her work and looked out the window at the stately courthouse *Texas Monthly* once proclaimed the prettiest town square in Texas. On a day like today, spring breathed across the land, whispering promises of flowers to come. Sesty didn't fall for it. She'd been raised in North Texas, knew the untrustworthy weather could snap in a second. Summer was the only reliable season. It got blistering hot in June and stayed that way through September.

Something else she wasn't going to fall for was the man strolling across the courthouse square headed straight for her office.

Her pulse did a little break dance.

Monkey pudding. She wasn't ready to see Josh again. Not yet. Not until she'd had time to sort out her feelings.

After Sheriff Hondo had admonished them for breaking curfew last night and sent them on their way, she spent the night tossing and turning and spinning scenarios she had no business spinning. Seeing Josh before she was ready to deal with him would only compound her confusion.

Get out of here.

She snatched up her purse and barreled for the door, hustling down the hallway toward the back staircase that exited into the alley, her sensible pumps tapping out a hollow rhythm against the aged boards.

"Sesty!" Josh called out from the front staircase just as she reached the rich oak banister in the back.

Crap. How did a man with a bum knee move so quickly? Was he part ninja?

"No time." She waved a hand at him over her head without turning to look. "Appointment. Gotta go."

"Hang on, we can walk and talk."

She didn't wait, plunged down the stairs, every nerve ending in her body throbbing with excitement and fear.

Josh clambered down the steps after her. The man just kept coming. "I need to talk to you."

What? Did he need an anvil to fall on him to realize she did not want to talk to him right now?

"Later. We'll talk later," she called, forcing cheeriness into her voice so he wouldn't know how unsettled he made her, then broke through the exit door and out into the alley.

She skirted a Dumpster, ignoring a fry cook from the neighboring restaurant who was lounging against the side of the building smoking a cigarette that did not smell entirely legal. The guy snubbed out his smoke, ducked back inside with a sheepish air.

And damn if Josh wasn't still following her. "About last night—"

Sesty stopped in the middle of the alley, turned back and raised a palm. "I have no memory of last night."

"Kiss amnesia, huh?" He smiled at her with a tenderness that almost stopped her heart. A grin bomb. Boom! He detonated it on her, knowing exactly what he was doing. He'd used it on her before, primarily the night he'd coaxed her out of her virginity.

Not that she'd been that hard to convince.

"What kiss?" She blinked rapidly, buying time to mentally vacuum ever speck of restraint she possessed as a force field against that smile.

"Denying it doesn't mean it didn't happen," he drawled, trying to reel her in with that sexy voice.

She folded her arms over her chest. *Knees, don't wobble now.* "Meaning what exactly?"

"Meaning . . ." He looked flummoxed.

"See? The kiss meant nothing. It was good. It was great. Okay, maybe the best damned kiss ever, but so what? In the grand scheme of things it doesn't mean a thing."

"It means there's something still there."

"Still where?"

"Between us."

"No it doesn't." It was getting really hard to breathe with him staring at her like that. So much for inner fortitude. She spun on her heels, stalked away.

His footsteps padded behind her.

"Stop it," she called over her shoulder.

"Stop what?"

"You're skulking. Stop skulking."

"Then stop running away and talk to me."

"Fine." She spun around, heaved a heavy sigh. "Talk."

"Apparently, I shouldn't have kissed you." He came closer.

"Okay, now we've got that straight, let's move on."

"I shouldn't have," he said, reaching out to grab her elbow before she could turn away again. The second he touched her, goose bumps froze her skin. "I shouldn't have, but I did."

"Look, this doesn't have to be a thing. Let's not turn it into a thing. We'll just shut up about it and move on."

"I don't want to do that," he insisted.

"But I do."

"Are you saying that your world was not rocked?"

"Yep. That's exactly what I'm saying," she said, nodding her head so vigorously her dangling earrings slapped against her neck. "No rocking going on. My world was not rocked. In fact, it was the opposite of rocked. My world is solidified in cement."

"After I kissed you."

"That's right." She wished he would let go of her elbow and stop looking at her like she was the cutest thing he'd ever seen.

"Then why did you invite me home with you?"

"Do I do that?"

He held up both palms. "My mistake. I thought since my world was rocked, yours was too."

Something shifted in his face, darkened his eyes. Disappointment? Her heart staggered, and it hit her with breath-stealing rawness that this man, once known only for being the cockiest daredevil in Hood County, was now a NASCAR star and she didn't stand a chance with him. Not long-term. Not for happily-ever-after, and that's all she'd ever wanted.

So here's the part where you just say hang it all and have wild monkey sex with him.

"Nope." She stubbornly hardened her chin. She could not let him back into her life. Soon as he was healed, he'd be back on that NASCAR track surrounded by adoring fans, zooming off without her. "Not rocked."

He inclined his head, his hair falling across his forehead. Why did he have to be so damn charming? "You sure about that?"

"Positive."

"Could it just be that you're scared, because it's understandable if you're scared. Your boyfriend cheated on you. He burned a hole through your heart. You're afraid if you let me in again, I'll hurt you too."

She notched up her chin. "I'm not afraid."

He stared at her so hard it set her head spinning. "Really? Because I am. I'm scared to death."

The vulnerability in his voice made her want to confess, tell him, *Hell yes, I'm scared. You scare the living daylights out of me, Josh Langtree, because if I let you, you could break my heart into a million little pieces.* He could hurt her so much worse than Chad ever had.

"You don't have to be scared," she said. "Don't worry

about it. This too shall pass. Fill in the blank with whatever platitude works for you. Nothing happened but a kiss. We didn't cross a line. No line was crossed," she blathered.

"But you wanted to cross that line. Last night. You invited me home with you."

"Momentary insanity."

He moistened his lips. His fingers were still locked around her elbow. Why wouldn't he let her go? "You're not the least bit curious—"

"No!" she said more emphatically than she intended.

"My mistake." His Adam's apple bobbled like he was going to say something more but changed his mind and swallowed back the words.

"Look . . ." She softened her tone. "It's complicated. You're on the rebound. I'm on the rebound. You're only in town for a few weeks. I'm here to stay."

"Who says it has to be anything more than a good time?"

Yes! Yes! Take me now! Her knees did start to wobble then. "I can't, Josh. Not with you. If I slept with you—"

"What?" he pressed. His hand was so warm.

"Nothing has really changed in ten years, has it? The same reason we didn't work then is the same reason we wouldn't work now."

"But the sparks are still there. You can't deny that."

"Phenethylamine. That's all it is."

"You're right." He smiled in a breezy way, but she wouldn't lay any bets on the authenticity of it. "Phenethylamine. That stuff really sneaks up on you." His short laugh was as undependable as the smile. "Twilight almost hooked me."

"Valentine's Day propaganda will do it to you every time. It's nothing to be ashamed of. Just as long as you come to your senses and shake it off." Her smile was as phony as his.

"You make an excellent point." He tightened his grip on her elbow the slightest little bit and then let go and stepped away.

It was all she could do to keep from stroking her fingers over the skin he'd just touched. "Besides, you're the hottest bachelor on the auction block. We don't want the ladies believing I've been sampling the wares. Gotta get those bids up. Holly's House is counting on you."

They stood there a moment, the rosy scent of the flowers from Caitlyn Garza's flower shop on the corner mingled with the odor of overripe Dumpster. One heartbeat. Two. Three.

"Where do we go from here, you and me?"

She straightened. The event planner. The professional. "You still owe me thirty-four hours of community service. Help break down the conference center after the bridal show is over tomorrow afternoon at five and set up for the bachelor auction on Saturday. That's where we go from here."

"And then?"

"There's the auction itself."

"And after that?"

"Why after that you'll be off on a date with the woman who buys you."

Chapter Seven

ON FRIDAY MORNING, February 14, eager brides-to-be from all around the Dallas–Fort Worth metroplex descended upon Twilight. Cars filled the conference center parking lot as fresh-faced young women rushed inside to visit the wedding vendors.

Around the town square, kiosks had been set up to take advantage of the holiday.

Flower carts sold roses; their crimson smell filled the air. Merchants peddled heart-shaped jewelry engraved with mushy quotes. Lovers could have personalized cards made while they waited. A clerk from the Candy Bin passed out samples of heart-shaped chocolate truffles. Perks had a sandwich sign parked on the sidewalk outside the shop: "Today's Special: Sweetheart Hot Chocolate Half Price."

Every B&B in town was full. Couples, both young and old, strolled arm and arm around the square. Soaking it up, smiling dopily at each other, resting heads on shoulders, falling hook, line, and sinker for Valentine's Day.

Ah, phenethylamine, that wicked, wicked stuff.

The morning started out sunny, but by noon the sky was overcast and the temperature had dropped fifteen degrees. Merchants scrambled to adjust, pulling out sweaters, wraps, gloves, and hats to sell.

By five o'clock, when the bridal show ended, the wind was whipping across the lake, making the fifty degrees feel like thirty. The sky was so dark it might as well have been midnight, and the local weathermen were calling for a tornado watch. Tornadoes in February weren't all that common, but they weren't unheard of either.

The previous year, a tornado had hit Twilight and lives were lost, and now everyone was edgy when it came to thunderstorms. Sesty counted herself lucky to have purchased a house that came equipped with a storm cellar in the backyard. But a tornado watch was only a watch. She couldn't let the threat of a maybe storm keep her from getting the conference center ready for tomorrow's auction.

She dashed from her office to the conference center, a short three blocks away, but in the dark and cold it felt much farther. The kiosks had vanished, but the restaurants on the square were lit up and she could hear laughter and warm conversation spilling out as she hurried past, collar upturned, head bent against the wind.

She arrived at the conference center to find Josh there with about twenty high school boys. They'd already broken down the vendor booths and were busy sweeping up. The cutouts she and Josh had built were stacked on the stage, ready to be arranged. Sesty stood in the doorway a moment, watching him with the kids.

As he and the teens moved the chairs back onto the conference center floor, Josh instructed the boys on car maintenance and safe driving techniques. They hung on his every word. She was mesmerized by him too—his depth of knowledge, how relaxed he was with the kids, the way the room just seemed brighter with him in it.

He looked up and caught her studying him. Instantly, his face warmed and he straightened, setting down the folding chair in his arms. "Here's the boss," he told the boys. "We're ready to start setting up for the auction. Tell us what you need for us to do."

"Everyone should go on home," she said. "I appreciate your help, but with the storm warnings, I don't want to be responsible for you kids getting caught out in it."

"But miss," one kid said, "Mr. Langtree was gonna take us out for pizza afterward."

"Miss Snow is right. We'll have to take a rain check." Josh clamped a hand on the teen's shoulder. "Quite literally. Sunday night. Pappa Pastas. I'll reserve the banquet room."

After a few disappointed mumbles and grumbles, the teens agreed and started arranging carpools to get home. Within a few minutes she and Josh were alone in the conference center.

"Wow," she said. "Where and how did you get the kids to help you? I thought it was going to take us hours to clear this place out, and you've already got it done. How did you manage it?"

"Many hands make light work."

"Even so . . ." She swept a hand at the empty room. "The bridal show went until five, and it's only . . ." She glanced at her watch. ". . . fifteen after."

"Because of the weather, the crowd thinned out around four, so most of the vendors left early."

"How did you get the set designs?"

"Your assistant asked me to bring them over."

Staring into his mesmerizing eyes, she could barely think. What was Jana up to? "And the boys?"

"I dropped by the high school this morning to see my old shop teacher, and he asked me to give a speech to the class. All it took was the promise of pizza and the boys were over here like a shot."

"It wasn't the pizza, Josh. It was you. Those kids look at you like you hung the moon and the stars and the Milky Way."

"They think it's cool I crashed a two hundred thousand dollar car. Little do they know . . ." He tapped his injured leg.

"Don't undersell yourself. You're good with them."

"Some might say it's because I'm as immature as they are."

"You're not." She cocked her head. "You're different than you used to be."

"Is that right?" His smile was Little Red Riding Hood wolfish.

"You're . . ." She canted her head, sized him up. Long and lean in his blue jeans and T-shirt, so similar to the boy he'd been, and yet, not.

"What?" he nudged.

"You've wised up."

"Now that's the kiss of death." He put an index finger to his lips. "Shh, don't tell the kids."

"In spite of the racing and the wrecking, you've got a head on your shoulders."

"Ah, Ses, don't get all serious on me."

"I mean it. I didn't realize it at first because you're so good at the cool, cocky dude thing, but the celebrity stuff didn't go to your head. I'm impressed."

"Oh, but it did. Be glad you weren't around to see that. You would have hated me."

"I could never hate you, Josh."

"But you can't lo—" He broke off, shook his head.

What had he been about to say? Her pulse thumped wildly. Her chest suddenly seemed too small and her heart too big. "Is something bothering you?"

He put a hand to the nape of his neck, shifted a sidelong glance at her, opened his mouth, shut it again, hesitated.

"What is it?" she prompted, uncertain whether she wanted to hear what he had to say.

His hand moved to shove a lock of hair from his forehead, a boyish gesture accompanied by a cheery, photoshoot smile and a no-big-deal shrug that belied the weariness in the back of his eyes.

Something *was* bothering him. "Josh?"

"I don't know whether it was the wreck or Miley screwing around on me or maybe that thirty is looming in my windshield, but as much as I love what I do, stardom doesn't live up to fantasy."

"A case of 'I got everything I've ever wanted and I'm still not happy'?"

"Don't get me wrong, I wouldn't trade the life I've had for anything, but it's not the summit people think it is."

"See, you have changed. The seventeen-year-old Josh would have said you are out of your freaking mind."

"Don't forget that seventeen-year-old Josh drove off and left you in his rearview mirror."

Her heart filled up her chest, taking every spare inch of room, leaving her a little dizzy. They stared at each other for the length of time it took her swelling heart to beat once, twice, three times.

Josh cleared his throat and drew an envelop from his back pocket. "I got something for you."

"That's not a Valentine's Day card, is it?"

"Absolutely not."

She felt at once relieved and slightly sick in her stomach. "Oh, good. That's great. What is it?"

"Open it up."

A vein at her temple ticked hot as she slid her finger underneath the flap of the envelope and removed the card. It was handmade from black construction paper and decorated with a white upside down heart on the front. The lettering was in red fingernail polish.

Because we both hate all that phenethylamine Valentine's Day stuff . . .

"It's stupid. Give it back." He grabbed for it.

She held it behind her. "No, you gave it to me, it's mine."

He reached around her, his body brushing up against hers. Instant tingles poked her nerve endings like cactus spines and she jumped back. "Don't open it."

She opened up the card to find a strip of vacuum-sealed bacon had been taped there.

Here's some meat.

She looked up at Josh. His forehead was wrinkled and he was leaning forward, both hands shoved into his pockets. Aww. He was anxious about her reaction.

"I just realized the line about meat makes me sound like a total tool. I didn't mean it that way. I was trying to think of something that was the opposite of chocolate, and bacon came to mind, clearly I did not fully think this through."

"You thought I would be offended by a meat reference?" Slowly, she dropped her gaze to his crotch. The man had a full-on erection. Oh, my. She slung her gaze back to his face.

He hitched his fingers through his belt loops. "You're not?"

"It's hysterical. The perfect Valentine's Day card for Valentine's haters the world over. Thank you."

"Glad you like it." His gaze locked on her lips, and she just knew he was about to kiss her again and she was going to let him.

The lights flickered. Outside, the wind howled. The moment was lost.

"We should be getting home too," he murmured.

"I can't. I have to set up for the bachelor auction. It's—"

"If a tornado hits there will be no bachelor auction. It's not worth risking your life over."

"What are the odds it will hit here?"

"When it comes to your safety, any odds are too high."

"Says the daredevil NASCAR driver."

He touched her shoulder, and her body lit up like a circuit board. "Ses, I'll get up early, get the boys back here. We'll have it decorated in an hour. Stop sweating the small stuff."

"But that's my job, Josh, to sweat the small stuff."

"And mine is to make sure you get home safely."

"Says who?"

"Says me."

She was about to argue, but he was right. Why give him grief over it?

"Where'd you park?" he asked.

"I didn't. I walked."

"Do you ever take a car?"

"I live half a mile from my office," she said. "Most all the events I plan are on or around the town square. Walking is good exercise."

"Not in a winter thunderstorm it's not."

"Okay, I'll give you that."

"C'mon," he said, and hooked his arm around her waist. "I'll drive you home."

HE WAS IN the car.

Alone.

With Sesty.

He hadn't been here in ten years. His loss.

The confines of his black classic Chevy Camaro smelled like her—a sweet, womanly scent jettisoning him back in time.

She looked so beautiful in the glow of the dashboard light he almost got choked up. Yesterday she'd made it clear in no uncertain terms that she was not interested in starting anything up again, and she had good points against it.

He didn't give a damn. He wanted her anyway.

And she wanted him too. The kisses they'd shared in Sweetheart Park didn't lie. What would it take to convince her he was serious about this? About her?

Wind slammed against the car, demanding and relentless. Rain battered the windshield. It was shaping up to be one helluva storm.

Josh gripped the wheel. Eyes on the road. Head in the game. Get her home safely.

"Oh gosh," she fretted, and bit down on a thumbnail. "I might not be a big fan of Valentine's Day, but I didn't want it to end in a real disaster."

"Don't borrow trouble," he soothed, but switched on the radio in search of a weather report.

A stern-voiced weatherman cautioned, "The counties of Hood, Parker, and Erath are under a tornado warning. Please take shelter."

"All I can think about is that tornado that hit Twilight last year. I hope those kids all got home okay. I don't think I could live with myself if something happened to them." She wrung her hands.

Josh reached across the seat, laid a palm on her shoulder. "Breathe. It will be okay."

"You don't know that."

"It's not a disaster until it's a disaster. In the meantime it's just a learning experience."

"Wisdom gleamed from the track."

"Yeah."

"And if it is a disaster?"

"We deal with it when and if it happens. If we spend all our time worrying about what may never come, we don't ever live fully in the moment."

"This moment is scary enough," she said. "I don't really want to live fully in it."

He returned his hand to the wheel and pulled into her driveway. "We're here."

Just as they stepped from the car, everything stopped.

No wind. No rain. The eerie stillness raised the hairs on the back of his neck.

"Uh-oh," Sesty whispered at the same time the civil defense sirens went off.

"We've got to get into the house." He grabbed her hand, dragged her toward the front door.

"Wait." She balked.

"Don't make me pick you up and carry you, woman," he growled. "You don't always have to be in control."

"Listen to me. I have a storm cellar," she said. "This way."

He followed her into the backyard. The streetlights were still on but the sky was completely black. Sesty led the way through her backyard gate and to the underground storm shelter.

The snap of the cellar door cut off the ear-bruising shriek of alarm sirens and splashed them in total darkness. Sesty descended the steps ahead of him, leaving Josh to duck his head to keep from whacking into the low-ceilinged entrance. He ran a hand along the wall, feeling his way down.

The blackness was complete. Not a glimmer of light anywhere.

He heard her stumble, grunt. "You okay?"

"Tripped," she said.

"You got flashlights or candles stored in here?"

Her voice came back to him, tinny and high. "I was supposed to. I meant to, but I never got around to it."

"You? Little Miss Organized?" He feigned sounding scandalized.

"I've only been living here four months," she said defensively.

"No judgment. Do you have your cell phone on you? We can use that for light. I left mine in my car."

"Mine's in my purse. In your car."

"No worries," he said. "Tornadoes don't last long."

His foot contacted with the bench and his knee brushed against hers. She sucked in her breath and quickly moved her knee. He sank down onto the seat beside her, heard her shifting around in the darkness.

The room was tiny, designed for six people max, and that was only if they were smashed in tight. It was pretty damn cozy with just the two of them, and he couldn't say he really minded being down here with her, concerns about the storm aside.

The siren's scream was muffled; it seemed far away, in another land, another time. The roar of the wind rushing above them was far away too. They were in here together. They couldn't be harmed.

Her hand touched his in the dark; a small, delicate hand; the first hand he'd ever held as a lover, and her warm fingers curled around his palm. He closed his hand around hers, squeezed it gently.

She sighed lightly and rested her head against his shoulder.

Josh felt the moment deep inside him, not just physically, but emotionally and, yeah, damn, he was just going to admit it, spiritually. The expanding energy flooded his body, heated his pores, whooshed through his bloodstream. It fueled his cells, glands, sinew, and bones, zipping and zooming, gathering speed until it crashed with a halting shudder squarely in the middle of his chest.

She was his first love, and he wanted her to be his last, and there was no one else he'd rather be hunkered in a storm shelter with on Valentine's Day than Sesty.

HIS LIPS FOUND hers, sonar in the darkness.

Hard. His kiss was hard and so was his body.

Their breaths mingled. Warm plus warm equaled blistering. His hands came up to cup her face. Rough calluses stroked the soft skin of her cheeks, and he tilted her head, giving him deeper access.

She inhaled sharply, drawing in his scent, enriching the taste of him on her tongue and spurring a rash of goose bumps breaking out across her chest.

He made a gruff male noise, half grunt, half groan, causing her pulse to dash so fast she grew dizzy. Good thing he was wrapping those muscular biceps around her. Or maybe it wasn't such a good thing because now any resistance she might have been able to muster was crushed.

All she wanted to do was let go and *feel*.

This moment. This man. This magnificence.

He drew her into his lap and she didn't even whimper a protest. What was there to protest? Being here together seemed fated, and she wanted him. Wanted him more than she wanted to breathe.

So let him know.

She raised her hands. She couldn't see a thing, but she didn't need to. His body was familiar territory and she'd explored it before.

But as she ran her hands around the back of his neck, searching the provocative terrain, her seeking fingers discovered fresh landmarks—a ridge of a scar at the base of his nape, bulkier muscles bunching beneath her touch, shoulder blades once thin and sharp, now thicker, more solid.

He was changed and the familiar was suddenly foreign.

Her butt was planted across hard, broad thighs and she could feel the strain of denim over his erection. Her fingers played in his hair, ah, something that hadn't changed, the shape of his head. Here, she knew him.

Lightly, he bit her bottom lip with the nip of his teeth

and her whole body went pliant, hot and wet with perspiration and need. Everywhere his fingers touched, her skin burst into little flames.

Her eyes were open but the blackness in the cellar was absolute. She might as well have had her eyes squeezed tightly closed.

He was panting, but so was she. Even so, he kept kissing her, his tongue invading her—hallelujah—aggressively masculine and fully in control. If he drove like he kissed, look out Dale Earnhardt, Jr.

Her nipples turned to pebbles inside her bra and a moan leaked from her lungs.

His arm tightened around her waist, holding her captive, but she was no prisoner, and she wasn't going anywhere, storm or no storm.

A deep, overwhelming ache lodged between her legs, and she wanted him, oh how she wanted him. But this wasn't how she'd pictured their reunion. Okay, yes, dammit, ever since he'd rocketed back into town, she'd been fantasizing about this happening in a soft bed with pillows, fresh sheets, and mood music.

She wrenched her mouth from his, broke the kiss.

"What is it?" he gasped.

"Josh, I—"

"I want you, Sesty, and I thought you wanted me too, even though you said you didn't, the looks you gave, the way you kissed me . . . did I read the messages wrong? Please don't tell me I read misread the signals, because—"

"You didn't misread the signals," she admitted. "I want you too."

"Okay." His breath was raspy. "What's the problem?"

"I wanted it to be perfect. Not some tornado-fueled lust-fest in a storm cellar."

"There you go with perfection again. Life isn't perfect, Ses. It's messy and complicated and sprawling. If you're gonna take the ride, you've got to expect some potholes and sharp curves and loose stuff on the apron."

"What?"

"Race term, means debris on the unpaved portion of the track, but never mind that. The point I'm trying to make is that smooth rides are boring as hell. If everything is perfect and you know what's up ahead, then where's the excitement, where's the adventure?"

She plucked at the collar of his shirt, feeling the tension in his body. "I'm scared."

"Of what?"

"That I won't be very good. I'm not . . . I haven't had a lot of lovers."

"I thought you had scads."

"I lied. You're used to sophisticated women who know things."

"You know things."

"Not bedroom things."

"You know more than you think." He nuzzled her neck. "You'll be fine. We'll be fine together."

"And if we're not?"

"Practice makes perfect." He chuckled. "So we'll just have to keep trying."

"But—"

"Hush," he said gently. "What else are you afraid of?"

"Who says I'm afraid of anything else?"

"Your tight muscles."

She took a deep breath of this hair. It smelled so good.

"Sesty . . ."

"I'm afraid . . ." She cleared her throat. ". . . we'll flame out."

"Whenever you take a chance on something there's always the risk it won't work out." He sounded so matter of fact, as if it were easy to clean up the mess after a spill.

"Like you and Miley?"

"And you and Chad."

"Not like me and Chad, we were barely a thing. Just getting started. He made me mad more than anything else."

He didn't say anything about how much Miley had hurt him. That probably meant his ex had scarred him deeply. They had been engaged, after all. Sesty swallowed and tried not to think about that.

"You and me, we got started from our first date, remember?" Josh said.

"How could I forget? Picnic on the old suspension bridge. You brought my favorite snack cake."

"They were my favorite too."

She sighed.

"What is it?" he wheedled softly.

"I just keep thinking that if I'd done things differently, been better, worked harder, then you and I, we . . ."

"What? That we would have lasted?"

"Yes," she admitted in a small voice.

"Don't put that on yourself. We were young. Still kids."

"But I loved you so much back then."

He squeezed her tighter. "It was a tough time, yeah. But you had college and I had a dream. Our parents were against getting together. I was reckless, and as my grandfather liked to say, full of piss and vinegar, and when it all came to a head and you told me it was over, my heart shattered like glass. But you know, I learned a lot and grew up and now I'm back and we want each other as much now as we did then. Hell, even more. I want you more."

"Your heart shattered?"

"Like a windshield hitting a wall at ninety miles an hour."

"Aren't you afraid that I'll break it again?"

"Absolutely, but you gotta risk failure to reap the rewards."

"So you keep saying."

"You think too much," he said, and burned a kiss along her jaw. "Always have."

"But I want to do this right. I don't want to screw it up this time. I want to be—"

"If you say perfect, I'm calling the whole thing off," he threatened.

"Really?"

"Really."

Seconds ticked by, but he never loosened his grip on her.

"You're not going to say it?" he asked.

She shook her head, even though she knew he couldn't see her.

"Do you want to do this? Here? Now? You've got to say it."

"I want you," she whispered, "but we don't have any protection. And that's one part of perfect I can't let go of."

"Honey," he said, "there's a condom in my wallet in my back pocket. Sex is one place where you should leave the perfection to me."

"That sounds kind of braggy."

"Just stating the facts." He was touching her in places that instantly set her ablaze. His fingertips were hot as bottled lightning. Lust fired between her legs and she surrendered. Gave up perfection. Let go of control. Let him take the wheel.

When his hands slipped between her thighs, she parted her legs and allowed him in. Their joining was sweet reunion, a fierce homecoming, vibrant sex more wonderful than ever the second time around.

He whispered her name. Once. Twice. A dozen times.

They melted into each other, their vision lost. But they didn't need to see. They knew each other so well, by touch and taste, smell and sound.

He rocked into her and she made a soft noise of pleasure, clung tightly to his neck. His fingers knotted in her hair, his energy blazing as ferociously as her own.

While this joining might be imperfect. No freshly showered bodies. No soft bed. No candles. No music besides the drumming of rain on the cellar door.

It was indeed the perfect anti–Valentine's Day.

Chapter Eight

"Wow." JOSH BREATHED into the darkness, Sesty tucked beside him as they lay on their backs on the hard plastic bench seating. "That was . . . Wow."

"Did I . . . was it . . . okay?" she asked, sounding so nervous that he almost laughed out loud instead of just grinning like a fool in the darkness.

"Okay? Okay? Hell no, it wasn't okay."

"I'm so sorry—"

"Don't you dare apologize," he said, and hauled her onto this bare chest. "It was the best sex of my life, bar none."

"You're not just saying that to make me feel good?"

"Woman, are you that blind?" he growled.

"Well, it *is* kind of dark in here."

Her anxiety about her performance was endearing, but then a panicked thought occurred to him. What if it had been bad for *her*? "You had a good time, right?"

"You blew my mind."

He hugged her tight, kissed the tip of her nose. She felt so warm and real. This. This right here was what had been missing from his life. A dream come true. She lowered her head, rested her cheek against his heart. The world felt full of possibilities.

But Miley had done a number on his heart and he wasn't sure he could trust his feelings. Maybe sex with Sesty had been so great simply because she was so familiar, part of his past, the comforts of coming home. Could she also be part of his future?

He wanted that, more than he could say, but were these feelings real? Could he trust them? Was she feeling for him what he was feeling for her? What if she wasn't?

Where did they go from here?

Idly, she twirled an index finger through his chest hairs, sighed sweetly, and he was seventeen all over and in love for the first and only time.

And then, to keep from thinking too much, he made love to her again, taking possession of her sweet body, slipping into her welcoming warmth, sliding home. Ah, traction—what every driver yearned for.

Except along with traction came commitment. Once you were in, you were committed. Yeah, well, maybe it was time he committed to something besides racing.

Half an hour later she was curled into his lap, his head propped against the wall. She'd blown his gaskets.

"Do you think the storm has passed?" she whispered.

"The one outside or the one in here?"

She giggled and rubbed her nose against the underside of his chin. What a great sound!

"Let's listen," he said.

For a long moment they lay there listening and absorbing each other's body heat.

"I don't hear anything," she ventured.

"Me either."

"What time is it, do you suppose?"

He had no idea. It might have been minutes since they came into the cellar, or it could have been hours. He'd been so into her nothing else registered.

She sat up. "Should we go investigate?"

He wanted to say no. Wanted to stay here with her until the end of time. Just the two of them making love forever and ever.

"I suppose," he murmured.

"It's going to be a chore finding our clothes in the dark."

"Good thing it's a small space."

Several minutes later they located their clothing, got dressed, and headed up the steps, Josh leading the way as he held Sesty's hand tightly. He hated the idea of letting go of her.

He opened the cellar door hatch and a brittle damp wind slapped him in the face. Immediately, he drew Sesty to his side, tucking her against his body to shield her from the cold.

It was almost as black outside the cellar as it had been beneath the earth. The streetlights had gone out and the houses were dark, but overhead a sprinkling of stars glittered through the parting clouds.

Sounds of swift water swelled throughout the night.

Sesty's neighborhood was in a low spot, and flash flooding from the river tributary that fed into Sweetheart Park was a real possibility. How much rain had they gotten?

"Listen," she said, and put a hand to his shoulder. "Do you hear that?"

He cocked his head, strained to hear above the rushing water. Faintly, hoarsely, he could hear a woman calling for help.

Sesty gripped his bicep. "Josh, someone is in trouble."

THEY DROVE TO the low water crossing near Sweetheart Park, the headlights of Josh's Camaro picking up the reflection of a white sedan stranded in the middle of the crossing. Only the roof of the sedan was visible above the swirling current. And sitting on that sparse piece of roof, inches from being swept away in the water, huddled a young woman.

The woman saw them, rose to her feet, waving her arms over her head. "Help! Help!"

Sesty clasped a hand to her throat. "Oh my God, it's Jana."

As they watched, stunned, the current picked up the car and swirled it around like it was a leaf. Jana staggered, fell to her knees, pure terror on her face.

"Josh, Jana can't swim!"

"Call 911," he yelled, and jumped from the Camaro that he'd parked on the rise above the water.

She tumbled out of the car too, her heart taking the express elevator to her throat.

With trembling fingers it took her three tries to successfully get 911 punched into her cell phone between frightened peeks at the drama playing out a few yards away.

Jana clung to the roof, the sedan caught in a perverse ballet.

Josh kicked off his shoes at the water's edge. He was going in.

"Don't!" Sesty cried, but she knew she could not stop him. "Wait for backup," she added in a useless whisper.

He dove into the icy water, and the harsh *splat* his body made hitting the surface drove a physical pain into the dead center of her gut. She heard him grunt out loud.

The white sedan pitched again, dumping Jana into the water as she let out an abbreviated scream. Josh battled the current, struggling to reach her.

Sesty hopped up and down. The current was too swift! They were both going to drown right before her eyes. *No, no, please God, please God, no!*

A wail of sirens cut the air.

Help was on the way.

But too late?

Jana had disappeared from view. And Josh? He plunged beneath the surface where Sesty had last seen her assistant.

She chewed her fingernails, searching the black water for any sign of them in the headlight beams, and counted off the seconds—one, one thousand, two, one thousand. It felt like a year.

In a stream of strobe lights, fire trucks and ambulances blasted to a halt behind the Camaro. Instantly, firemen flowed around her, just as Josh broke the surface of the water, Jana clutched in his arms.

ONCE HIS FEET touched the ground, Josh's throbbing knee would not support him. He stumbled with Jana in his arms, pitched forward. A fireman took the terrified girl from him and Josh slumped sideways in the water, the wrenching pain in his knee setting his nerve endings on fire.

He'd known the second he hit the water that the impact reinjured his healing knee, but the adrenaline pumping through his body prevented him from thinking about it.

Until now.

Two firemen had hold of him and were dragging him to an awaiting ambulance. Sesty hovered behind them, her face sickly pale.

"How's Jana?" he croaked.

"Looks like she has hypothermia," said one of the firemen. "She was on top of the car for over an hour in freezing weather and then in the water. It was damn foolish, jumping into a raging current like that, but if you hadn't . . ." He shook his head.

Josh winced when the firemen boosted him into the ambulance. Winced again when the awaiting paramedic guided him to lie down on the stretcher.

"You're hurt!" Sesty exclaimed climbing up beside.

"Ma'am, please get down," the paramedic said gruffly.

"It's okay," Josh said. "She's with me."

"Don't get in the way," the paramedic cautioned her, and reached for a blood pressure cuff.

It was only then that Josh realized his body was shaking so hard the paramedic could hardly get the cuff wrapped around his arm.

"What's wrong with him?" Sesty asked the medic, anxiety twisting her pretty face into a mask of worry.

"Hypothermia is a concern. We'll know more when we get him to the hospital."

He must have dozed off, Josh realized, because the next thing he knew he was in the emergency room. His soaking wet clothes had been stripped off of him and a pile of heated blankets stacked atop him. Sesty stood at his side, holding his hand.

"What happened?" he asked.

"You blacked out there for a while. They said it's not uncommon in cases of hypothermia."

"Jana?"

"She's going to be okay. You saved her life, Josh. I never thought I'd say this, but I'm so glad you're a daredevil. Given the circumstances, most people would not have jumped into that water to save her."

"I just acted on instinct. Didn't give it a thought."

Sesty squeezed his hand. "I'm so proud of you."

"Hey, hey, don't cry." He reached over to wipe a tear from her eye, and his knee kicked up a protest. He fell back against the pillow. Dammit.

"I'm just relieved you're okay."

"Did you hear anything about the tornado?" he asked,

changing the subject, unable to look at her misty eyes or, hell, he might get choked up himself. "How much damage was done?"

"We were lucky," she said. "A weak tornado touched down on ranchland north of town. Twilight had some trees knocked down from high winds and the flash flooding, but beyond you and Jana, nobody was hurt and property damage was minimal."

A technician in blue scrubs pulled back the curtain separating him from the other bays. Behind the woman loomed a portable X-ray machine that he recognized on sight. This wasn't his first rodeo. He'd been in more hospital emergency rooms than he could count.

"I'm here to X-ray your knee," the technician said.

"I'll be back." Sesty let go of his hand and moved away with a smile that sent his stomach crawling up inside his chest. "I'm going to check on Jana. She doesn't have any family here."

Neither do I, he wanted to say, but didn't.

The technician X-rayed his knee and departed. He stared up at the ceiling, wondering just how badly he'd screwed himself up this time and imagined what the owner of his NASCAR would say to more delay in him getting back on his feet. He wasn't the owner's only driver of course, but he was primary.

Was.

The longer he was out, the more difficult it was going to be to return.

While he'd been longing for more than life on the

road, aching for something substantial, he wasn't sure he was truly ready to hang up his driving gloves. But the decision might have already been taken out of his hands.

The curtain parted again. This time it was a petite, cocoa-skinned, raven-haired woman in green scrubs and a white lab coat with *Dr. Singh* embroidered across the left front pocket. Sesty was behind her.

The doctor introduced herself and then said, "I have reviewed your X ray. You have reinjured your knee."

"Yeah, I kind of figured that. How bad is it?"

"You are back at square one on your recovery." The doctor shook her head.

"Kind of figured that too."

"You will have to wear a knee brace for several weeks. I want to hold you overnight for observation and to have the brace fitted," Dr. Singh said. "I'll have a nurse wheel you up to a room."

"Can I stay with him?" Sesty asked the doctor.

"Are you family?" Dr. Singh asked.

"No, but he doesn't have any family in town."

Josh touched her forearm. "I'll be fine on my own. You have to get ready for the bachelor auction tomorrow. Go home and try to get some sleep."

"To hell with the auction," Sesty declared. "You come first."

He knew how much it meant to her that the auction to go off without a hitch. "I'm not arguing with you about this. Go. Take care of business."

"You *are* my business. You saved my assistant's life tonight."

"All the more reason for you to go. Jana won't be there to help you run the event."

"I'll call off the auction."

"And disappoint Holly's House? No way."

Her shoulders slumped in defeat. She knew he was right. "Is this what we get for blowing raspberries at Valentine's Day? Cupid exacts a mean revenge. Even if I do manage to pull off this auction, what good is it without our most eligible bachelor?"

"Hey, Doc." Josh shifted his gaze back to the doctor. "Once I have a brace on, is there any reason I can't walk up on stage at the bachelor auction tomorrow afternoon?"

Dr. Singh pursed her lips and furrowed her brow. "How long will you be standing?"

"Ten minutes tops," he vowed. "I'll sit for the rest of the event."

The doctor shook a chiding finger. "Ten minutes and not a second more."

He beamed at Sesty. "See? Everything will be fine."

"Seriously, Josh," Sesty protested. "I don't want you to risk it. We'll be fine without you."

"But then, your auction wouldn't be perfect with only eleven bachelors."

She threw her hands in the air. "Who cares about perfection?"

"You do."

"A wise man once told me there's no such thing as perfection, so why set myself up for failure?"

"I'm going to be there," he insisted. "Count on it."

She shook her head vehemently. "No. Not at the expense of your health, and besides, it won't be perfect anyway with you in a brace."

"Afraid a bum knee will bump down my asking price like a dented showroom appliance?" he teased.

"I'm afraid you'll make things worse by pushing yourself too hard too soon. This is your career we're talking about. If your knee doesn't heal properly, your NASCAR days could be over."

Good point.

Dr. Singh folded her arms over her chest and gave them an I-don't-have-time-for-this look. "Why don't you both get a good night's rest and discuss it in the morning?"

"There's nothing to discuss," Sesty said.

"Yeah, because I'll be there."

"Josh—"

"No arguments," he said, and pointed toward the small gap in the curtain. "Go."

She hardened that sexy little chin of hers and dug in her heels. "No."

If she was going to be stubborn, then he would have to be a hard-ass for her own good. "Don't you get it? We're not family. You're not my girlfriend. I don't need you here."

A flash of hurt flickered in her eyes and was like a knife to his heart, slicing mean and clean, and it was all he could do not to apologize immediately and retract his declaration, but he needed her to go while he sorted out a few things.

Her back stiffened and she gave a curt nod. " Fine. I'll see you tomorrow afternoon."

Don't fret, honey. I'll make it you up to you soon enough. Still, it killed his soul to have to hurt her, even for a little while.

As she disappeared behind the curtain, Josh started making telephone calls.

Chapter 9

SESTY DIDN'T SLEEP a wink. Instead of going home, she
went to the conference center and set up for the bachelor
auction all by herself. She finished not long after dawn
and took herself to breakfast at Virgil's Diner.

Even at that early hour, even in the wake of a torna-
dic near miss, even though it was February fifteenth, love
was still in full bloom in Twilight.

The chalkboard menu advertised the weekend special—
heart-shaped hotcakes, scrambled-up-in-love eggs, be-my-
Valentine bacon. The bacon made her think about Josh
and the anti–Valentine's card he had given her, and she
had to press the back of her hand against her nose to keep
from crying.

An elderly couple, whose fiftieth wedding anniver-
sary Sesty had planned the month before, were sitting in
a corner booth, holding hands under the table and gazing
into each other's eyes. At the checkout counter, the ca-

shier's husband donned his coat and kissed her on his way out the door.

And there was Chad, coming into the diner, his arm thrown around the barista from Perks.

They even had the audacity to wave.

Sesty smiled and waved back. She didn't care about Chad. Josh was the one breaking her heart.

It had always been Josh. She fell in love with him when she was seventeen and she'd never fallen out.

The waitress brought her coffee and took her food order. She was stirring cream into her cup when someone plunked into the seat across from her. For one second her heart skipped a beat.

Josh?

But no, it was Jana. Looking surprisingly chipper considering what she'd been through.

"What are you doing out of the hospital?" Sesty asked.

"Are you kidding? I hate hospitals. As soon as I was warmed up, I was out of there." Jana snapped her fingers.

The waitress set Sesty's breakfast in front of her, took Jana's order, and moved on.

"How are you feeling?"

"With my hands," Jana deadpanned.

"You never did tell me how come you were out in the middle of the night in the aftermath of a tornado," Sesty said.

Jana feigned bewilderment. "I didn't?"

"No."

"Um . . . I might have taken advantage of Todd's attraction to me."

"Todd, the stage manager?"

A smug smile yanked up the corners of Jana's lips. "Now don't get me wrong. I didn't trade sexual favors in exchange for him ironing out the union wrinkles. Rather, we decided to explore the chemistry *after* he proved so helpful."

"And?"

"Not a love match, but . . ." Jana wobbled her head from side to side. "I'd go back again, although maybe not during a tornado. Although who knows? Maybe the threat of being blown away at any minute was what made the sex so hot."

That startled Sesty. Could the storm have been the thing that made her connection with Josh so powerful? It was something a sensible woman would take into consideration.

Jana reached across the table to flitch a strip of bacon off Sesty's plate. "Do you mind? I'm starving."

"I thought you were vegan."

"Sometimes. Most of the time. When I didn't almost die in a flash flood. I woke up this morning thinking, 'Life is short. I need bacon.' So here I am."

Sesty folded her hands in her lap. "Then how come you didn't order your own bacon?"

"What?" Jana crunched the bacon, made a blissful face. "And look like a hypocrite? I'm still a vegan, this is just a near-death-experience thing."

Sesty rubbed a palm over her upper arm. "I get you leaving the hospital, but what are you doing running around town? You should be home recovering."

"I'm fine, and you're going to need help wrangling this auction. If we get anywhere near the number of people who've told me they're coming, it'll be standing room only. Gotta remember to double-check the auditorium's fire code occupancy rate."

"Three hundred and sixteen."

Jana's eyes widened. "Damn, you know your stuff, girlfriend."

"As much as I appreciate the thought, please eat your breakfast, and then go home to bed," Sesty said.

"Not gonna happen." Jana made a noise of appreciation when the waitress brought the Belgium waffles she'd ordered and reached for the blueberry syrup sitting tableside.

Sesty blew out her breath so forcefully her bangs ruffled. "You're as stubborn as Josh."

"That guy . . ." Jana raised an index finger on the hand she was using to douse her waffle with syrup. "Now he's a keeper and my hero. If you don't want him, toss him my way."

Sesty's stomach contracted and her chest flared so hot that she had to slip out of her jacket. "The question isn't whether I want him, but if he wants me."

"Oh, he wants you." Jana's dreadlocks shook in agreement. "I've seen the way that man looks at you."

"Me and a million other fan girls."

"Don't give me that. You mean something to him."

Oh yeah? Then why did he throw me out of the hospital last night? "Apparently not enough," she mumbled.

Jana cocked her head. "What happened?"

"Let's not talk about him. If you're really determined to work today, let's talk about the auction."

"Are you going to eat the rest of your bacon?" Jana asked.

"Be my guest." Sesty waved at her plate, but then looking at the bacon made her think of Josh again and thinking of Josh made her feel possessive. "No, I changed my mind, give it back."

Jana deposited the bacon back on Sesty's plate, dusted her hands together and muttered, "Stingy."

"Backsliding vegan."

"He hurt you, didn't he?" Jana asked softly.

"Chad?" Sesty shook her head.

"You know I'm talking about Josh."

Sesty bit down on her bottom lip to keep it from trembling.

Jana put her hand on Sesty's. "He's just your rebound from Chad. You'll be over him in no time."

Sesty met Jana's eyes. "How I wish that were the case, but the truth is, every man I've ever been with was a rebound from Josh. I've loved him since I was seventeen years old and I probably always will."

"Don't give up, there's always hope."

Hope. Yes, well, wasn't that what had gotten her into this situation in the first place?

TEN MINUTES BEFORE the bachelor auction started, three hundred sixteen women packed into the auditorium of the Twilight Conference Center—head count courtesy of Matt Clipper, one of the burly firemen who'd pulled Jana and Josh from the water the night before. It was indeed standing room only.

Sesty was in full event planner mode. With her tablet computer tucked under her arm, she surveyed the bachelors lined up backstage—everyone was present and accounted for and in costume except for Josh. He hadn't shown up after all.

She told herself that it was okay. That he'd smartly taken her advice and decided to stay home and rest. She'd just step up to the microphone and inform the audience of his accident. The auction would go off without him. It wouldn't be perfect, but there was only so much she could control.

And who knew? Maybe Jana was right. Maybe there was hope.

But she wasn't about to do any breath holding.

Sesty surveyed the men arranged in front of her, gave them last minute coaching on how to enter and exit the stage. She adjusted costumes, reminded them to smile, and then she knew she could delay no longer. It was time to get started.

She'd turned to the front of the auditorium to address the audience when the stage door opened. Josh appeared in the doorway wearing a cumbersome brace that went from his right ankle to his thigh, and he used crutches to propel forward.

Her heart clutched, stuttered. She rushed to hold the door open for him. Too nervous to look directly in his face, she stared at his hands, wrapped around the crutches.

"Didja give up on me?" he asked.

Her gaze moved up his forearms, clad in his NASCAR jacket, to the muscular bare chest beneath. Her lips burned. Last night her mouth had been all over that chest. He'd come looking the part. Even in a brace and crushes he was going to drive the women wild.

He drove *her* wild.

"No, I know you would come," she lied breathlessly.

"They had some trouble fitting me with the brace," he said. "Or I would have been here sooner."

At last she gathered the courage to look him in the face. The teasing light in his eyes had hope flaring inside her. Maybe . . . maybe . . .

"I've got to go get this thing started," she said. "Have a seat backstage. You're on last and you promised Dr. Singh you wouldn't be on your feet longer than ten minutes."

"Aye aye, Captain." He gave a jaunty salute.

Skin tingling, head dizzy, Sesty stepped around the curtain and onto the stage. She stared out at the sea of women and for one moment a wave of stage fright rushed over her. *Breathe.*

She stepped to the microphone and in a daze started her speech. She must have done all right because after she finished talking about Holly's House, the room burst into hearty applause. She turned the proceedings over to the auctioneer, stepped out of the limelight and headed back behind the scenes, where she felt most comfortable.

Stepping off the stage, she noticed something going on at the front door. As discreetly as possible, she scurried toward the front. The fireman stood at the open door between the lobby and the auditorium, blocking the way.

His arms were folded over his chest and he was shaking his head at a woman. All Sesty could see of her was blond hair.

"You have to let me in," she heard the woman say as she approached. "My fiancé is one of the bachelors and I need to bid on him before some bitch gets her claws into him."

"Sorry, lady. Fire code. No one else is getting in until someone leaves."

The blonde's voice grew strident. "Do you have any idea who I am?"

Sesty skirted around to the fireman's side. She'd never met the blonde but had seen pictures of her in magazines and on TV.

Miley Hunter.

And she was a hundred times more beautiful in person than in commercials. Miley possessed creamy flawless skin, a curvy but trim figure, mile long legs, and Angelina Jolie lips. She was, in a word, everything that Sesty was not.

Perfect.

Obviously, the woman was here to win Josh back.

Sesty's gaze dropped to the ring finger of Miley's hand. A three-caret, marquee-cut diamond sparkled there. All hope fled. If this woman wanted Josh back, she would get her way. Then an even worse thought occurred to her. What if Josh had called her and asked her to come to the auction? What if he wanted her there?

Oh God, she might just throw up.

"What's going on, Matt?" Sesty forced a smile and touched Matt's shoulder.

"Are you in charge?" Miley asked.

"I am."

"Will you please tell the incredible hulk here that I must get in? My fiancé is one of the bachelors—"

"Yes," Sesty said. "I heard you, but we're full to capacity."

Miley's eyes turned mean. "Until someone leaves. Make someone leave so I can come in."

Sesty had to bite her tongue to keep from telling the woman what a spoiled brat she was, but Miley was already causing enough of a scene. Heads were turning, women taking their attention off Ian, who was on the auction block. For the sake of Holly's House and the wonderful work they did there, she had to smooth this over.

"But of course," Sesty said. "I'll leave and you can come in, but let me forewarn you, there's no place to sit." She ducked under Matt's arm and stepped into the lobby.

"Shows how little you know me." Miley tossed her head and marched into the auditorium.

Sesty watched her go up to a woman on the back row and hand her a hundred dollar bill in exchange for her seat.

Dammit.

"That one's a brat," Matt said. "I don't care how beautiful she is. Pretty is as pretty does."

"She's used to getting her way."

"So why did you give in to her?" Matt asked.

"For the good of the event."

"Is she really Josh Langtree's fiancé?"

"She was until she cheated on him. I guess she's trying to win him back."

"Whew." Matt blew out his breath. "He's got a fire-brand on his hands with that one."

Firebrand.

Something she definitely was not.

Sesty stood in the lobby, observing the auction. More than anything, she wanted to get the hell out of here, but she was in charge. She'd see this through to the end.

It took an entire hour to get to the last bachelor. Number twelve.

Josh.

Hardly anyone had left the building. They'd come to see—and bid on—their homegrown NASCAR star. As she watched the women go into a bidding frenzy over the man she loved, it occurred to Sesty that she never stood a chance with Josh. He was too talented, too accomplished, just too damn hot for one woman.

She was out of her league and she knew it, as she'd known it at seventeen. Nothing had changed. He was still big-time and she was still small town.

This was the real reason she had let him go. Not because he was a daredevil. Not because her parents disapproved of him. But because she was scared she wouldn't measure up.

Fear.

That's what had been holding her back. Fear of loss, rejection, heartbreak. So she'd broken up with him before he'd broken up with her.

When Miley won the bidding, it was no surprise. She had the looks to intimidate the other women and the money to outbid them. What did surprise Sesty was that

Miley was willing to yell out, "Twenty-five thousand dollars!" when the previous bid had only been seven thousand.

That ended the auction on the spot, and the auctioneer called for Sesty to come back up onstage.

Matt pushed her forward and she walked up the aisle to thunderous applause. When Jana announced that they'd raised a total of forty-two thousand dollars, the crowd was on their feet by the time Sesty reached the stage.

A standing ovation.

For her.

It should have been a great moment. She'd achieved her goal. Done what she set out to do. Put together a perfect bachelor auction and funded the coffers of Holly's House so they could assist needy families get health care. Her event helped bring tourists into town, fill rooms at the B&Bs, and brought business to the restaurants and shops.

She should have been over-the-moon happy.

But in her peripheral vision, from where she was standing on stage, a plastic smile on her face, she could see Josh and Miley, who had her arms twined around his neck. Josh had his arms around Miley's waist and they were kissing as if it was the end of the world.

And that's exactly what it felt like to Sesty.

The end of the world.

Chapter Ten

SESTY WISHED SHE could flee the scene. Run home. Curl up in her bed and bawl her eyes out for being so stupid as to believe she could have a casual fling with Josh and it wouldn't come back to bite her in the butt.

How naïve she'd been for daring to hope.

But she had a job to finish and she could nurse her hurt later with a big bowl of Rocky Road ice cream.

And then?

Well, she'd worry about that later.

Current task? Oversee the cleanup at the conference center, pay the auctioneer, tie a bow in those picking-up-the-pieces tasks that followed a big event. All she had to do was concentrate, focus on the work and trust that keeping busy would scrub the image of Josh and Miley out on a hot date right out of her head.

Yeah, right. If you're buying that, there's this bridge in Brooklyn . . .

Through a mist of tears, she picked up the cutout of the bow-tied Valentine's Day teddy bear and carted it to the side of the stage, to the very spot where Josh had kissed Miley. The teddy bear he had cut out a second time to make it perfect for her.

Perfection.

There was no such thing. She knew it, and yet she kept trying to live up to impossible standards. Standards she'd imposed upon herself.

She heard the sound of the front door open. Blinking, she rubbed the tears from her eyes. Had someone forgotten something? Or had stubborn Jana come back again after she had insisted she go home and leave the cleanup to her.

For a moment she considered cowering behind the curtain, hoping the person would get what they came for and quietly leave, but then she scolded herself for being anti-social.

She peered around the curtain at the empty auditorium.

Except it wasn't empty.

Josh was propelling himself down the aisle on crutches, headed for the stage.

She dropped the curtain, plastered her back against the wall. Had he seen her? What was he doing back here? Had he come to tell her that he and Miley were back together? She held her breath, prayed he'd go away.

The sound of his crutches made a two-step thumping noise against the cement floor. "Sesty," he called. "I know you're back there."

"I'm busy," she hollered, and lightly pounded the back

of her head against the wall. Was he really going to make her do this? "And you have a date to get to."

"Come out here so I can talk to you."

"Nothing to talk about." She strove to keep her voice airy, carefree.

"I didn't know Miley was going to show up and bid on me."

Don't get sucked into a conversation about his perfect model fiancée. Don't do it.

"How did she find out about the auction in the first place?" Sesty cringed. *You just had to go and say it, didn't you?*

"Facebook."

"You're still friends with her on Facebook after the way she treated you?"

"It's a fan page, Sesty. Anyone can see it. I posted about the auction to help your event."

"Oh." Dammit. *Shut up talking, slide out the side door.*

"Are you going to make me climb those steps and come after you? Because I will," he threatened.

"I'm serious, Josh. There's nothing to discuss. Go have a happy life. I'm fine."

There was a long moment of silence where the only sounds she heard were the heater ducts blowing air and the hard pumping of her heart.

"I'm not," he said finally, in such a mournful tone that she peeked around the curtain again. He stood on the auditorium floor, just below the stage, the same place he'd stood when he stripped his shirt off for her that first day.

He dropped one crutch and it clattered to the floor,

braced the other crutch underneath his left arm and reached out a hand to her. "Come talk to me." He waited a beat and then added, "Please."

Her knees wavered, thin as water. She pressed a palm against the wall to steady herself.

Resist. You don't want to hear about his reconciliation with Miley

His smile guided her down the stage steps, but it was the smell of him—that particular blend of Lava soap and leather, licorice and man—that reeled her in. The scent was etched in her memory, forever burned there as *daredevil*. The walls of the auditorium seemed suddenly smaller, as if they were contracting inward.

She stopped three feet away from him, afraid that if she came any closer she'd fall on her knees and beg him to love her.

"Hey," he whispered.

"Where's your date?" she asked, even though she didn't really want to know.

"On her way back to Houston."

Sesty's lips formed an O, but no sound came out. There was that hope again, burning bright as an emergency flare.

"I sent her packing."

"She paid twenty-five thousand dollars for you."

"I told her I wasn't for sale and wrote her a check."

"You didn't make up with her?" Her pulse sprinted, hurtled.

"No."

"Why not?"

His eyes were welding torches, soldering his gaze to hers. "She wasn't you."

Sesty didn't move a muscle.

"That's the same thing Miley told me the night I caught her with my best friend. It was her excuse. She said during our relationship that I wasn't emotionally available because I was still hung up on you. She said it again just now as she drove away."

A fluttering started in the dead center of her chest. Hope was about to take wings and fly. She curled her hands into fists.

She stopped breathing. "You talked about me? To your fiancée?"

"Of course I did. You were my first, Sesty."

"I was *your* first?" She placed a palm to her chest. "You were a virgin too? When we did it the first time?"

"Made love, Ses. Go ahead and say the words, because that's what we did. We made love."

Was he talking about then or now? What did he want from her? How would she fit into his life?

"Before you go any further," she said, "there's something I have to tell you."

A look of alarm flared in his eyes. "Is it bad?"

"It all depends on you."

His hand was still outstretched, an invitation, beckoning her closer. She did not move.

"You hurt my feelings last night when you told me you didn't want me at the hospital. It made me feel cheap. Like once the sex was over, you were done with me."

"Sesty . . ." He shook his head, his eyes were so sad. "I never meant to make you feel that way."

"I know. It's my fault. I lied," she confessed. "I told you that I hated Valentine's Day, but it's not true. I love Valentine's Day. I love hearts and flowers and chubby babies flinging arrows. I love sappy cards and teddy bears that play "Sugar Pie, Honey Bunch" and candlelit dinners for two. I'm a sucker for all of it."

"I only said that about a no-strings-attached fling because I thought that's what you wanted."

She could hardly believe what she was hearing. "So what are you saying, Josh?"

"That Miley is right. I never fully got over you, and in fact, that's why I came back to Twilight. Not to heal, not to look after my grandmother's place, but to get to the bottom of my feelings about you."

"Really?" She breathed.

"I told you I didn't want you at the hospital because I knew you wouldn't leave if I didn't do something to make you go. I'm sorry I hurt you, and I intend on making it up to you the best way I know how." His gaze lingered on her lips. "But I needed time alone. I needed time to think."

"About what?" she asked so softly she could hardly hear herself.

He didn't immediately respond, and for a moment she thought he hadn't heard her, but then he dropped the second crutch and took a step toward her. The smacking noise as the crutch hit the floor echoed throughout the empty auditorium.

"To make the final decision about my future."

She gulped, moistened her lips, but she could not have broken her gaze from his face if a tornado had been barreling down on them. "What did you decide?"

"I'm done with NASCAR."

"Josh no! It's your heart and soul."

"Maybe it was once." He took another step toward her. "But it's not anymore."

"You're just saying that because you reinjured your knee. You'll think differently once it's healed."

Slowly, he shook his head. "I called the owner of the car I drive and told him I wouldn't be coming back."

She sucked in a massive gulp of air. Her head was spinning crazily out of control and she was trembling all over. "But wha . . . what are you going to do?"

"When I saw my old shop teacher, he told me he was retiring at the end of the school year and wants to start a local racetrack. He's got the land for it west of town and I've got the funds."

"You're opening a racetrack here in Twilight with your shop teacher?"

"It'll be small at first. Just somewhere kids can train."

She cupped her palms around her mouth. "Are you sure?"

"When you get to the NASCAR level, there's so much more going on than driving. It's all about money and competition. Don't get me wrong, I loved it, but now I want more. And I've always liked the basics of racing and I like teaching other people about the sport. You said yourself that I was good with kids."

She stared into his eyes and the world bloomed with possibilities.

"There's just one sticking point."

"What's that?"

"You, Sesty. None of this is worth a damn without you. I love you, Sesty. I never stopped loving you. Will you have me? I'm certainly not perfect, but I love you."

"Oh, Josh! I admit it. I fought against it, but there it is. I'm a fool for love." She gulped. "I'm a fool for you."

"Not a fool, not a fool at all."

He held his arms open wide and smiled the deepest, brightest smile she'd ever seen. A brilliant smile that said more than a million words ever could. His smile captured her, held her, promised a lifetime of love and kisses.

She flew into his arms and he wrapped them around her. It had taken them a decade to find their way back to each other, but there were some risks worth taking, and loving Josh was one of them.

Want more from *New York Times* bestselling author
Lori Wilde?

Read on for a sneak peek at

LOVE WITH A PERFECT COWBOY

The next fun and sexy installment in the
Cupid, Texas Series!

Available May 2014

AND

Don't miss the other
heartwarming novels in the
Twilight, Texas Series!

THE SWEETHEARTS' KNITTING CLUB
THE TRUE LOVE QUILTING CLUB
THE FIRST LOVE COOKIE CLUB
THE WELCOME HOME GARDEN CLUB
THE CHRISTMAS COOKIE COLLECTION

*Currently available in print and
ebook from Avon Books!*

Chapter One

New York, New York
April 1

MELODY SPENCER WAS rushing up Madison Avenue when she spied him.

A tall, lanky man in a black Stetson logjamming the flow of foot traffic by moseying along at a lamb's pace, craning his neck up at the skyscrapers as if he couldn't believe they made buildings that lofty.

Two simultaneous thoughts popped into her head. One was: *What a hick.* The other was: *I'm homesick.*

Twelve years earlier she had marveled at the towering buildings when she first arrived in the city as a green freshman on a full academic scholarship to NYU. While she no longer stared at the high-rises, she still lived by one motto—*Keep looking up.* Vision, commitment, and hard work were what had brought her to this moment.

She was about to receive the promotion she worked a lifetime to earn.

Why else would her boss, Michael Helmsly, have texted her and asked her to come in for a private meeting thirty minutes early on the same day that the creative director was retiring?

She shivered, smiled.

At long last her time had come.

A river of people flowed around the cowboy, some muttering obscenities, others flipping him off, a few glowering, but most not even bothering to acknowledge him at all. He was nothing more than a speck in their obstacle-laden day.

Although one smart-aleck teen—probably a tourist—hollered from a passing taxi, "Why aren't you naked in Times Square, cowboy?"

The man tipped his Stetson at the taxi, briefly revealing a head of thick, whiskey-colored curls and a sense of humor. A navy blue, Western-cut sport jacket hugged his broad shoulders. The crowd obscured her view of his backside, but she would have bet a hundred dollars that tight-fitting Wranglers cupped a spectacular butt.

Cowboys always seemed to have spectacular butts, probably from all that hard riding in the saddle.

He turned his head and the morning light illuminated his profile—straight nose, honed cheekbones, chiseled jaw. He was freshly clean-shaven, but she could tell he had a heavy beard and that long before five o'clock he'd be sporting a shadow of stubble. In that regard he looked a bit like the actor Josh Holloway, who'd played Sawyer on the television show *Lost*.

A cold jolt of recognition smacked into the pit of her stomach. She knew this man! Had once both loved and hated him.

Luke Nielson, from her hometown of Cupid, Texas.

Her chest tightened and suddenly she couldn't breathe. What was Luke doing in New York City attracting attention like the proverbial fish out of water? What if their eyes met and he recognized her?

Pulse thumping illogically fast, Melody ducked her head and scurried to the far side of the sidewalk. She had no time or inclination to take pity on him and help him navigate the city. He was on his own.

Coward.

She had fifteen minutes to spare. She was using the meeting as an excuse to get away from him. Right-o. And a good excuse it was. She needed those few minutes to compose her thoughts and tamp down her excitement before heading into her boss's office. Cool, calm, and unruffled. That was the image she projected on the job.

Praying that Luke hadn't seen her, she held her breath until she put an entire city block between them. By the time she exhaled, her lungs felt stretched and achy. Okay, she dodged a bullet, onward and upward.

She pushed through the frosted glass door of the building that housed the Tribalgate offices. In the lobby, the security guard positioned at the check-in desk nodded a mute greeting as Melody used her ID badge to swipe her way through the turnstile granting access to the elevators.

Because she was a bit early, there was no one else waiting for the elevator to the thirty-fourth floor. On the ride up, she whipped out her cell phone to text her boyfriend.

Jean-Claude was a top-tier photographer who traveled all around the world, and Melody still couldn't believe he'd chosen her when he had his pick of beautiful, fascinating women. Yes, sometimes he was distant and a bit self-absorbed, but what artist wasn't? He might not be the love of her life, but they had a nice thing going on.

For the last two weeks, she'd been living with Jean-Claude in his Upper West Side apartment across from Central Park. Not to mention that her new residence and illustrious boyfriend had duly impressed her mother, Carol Ann Fant Spencer, when she told her about him, although her mother had immediately made when-are-you-getting-married noises.

It was definitely a monumental step up from her former loft apartment in Queens, although moving in with Jean-Claude had taken a nerve-wracking leap of faith on a relationship that was barely two months old. But her landlord had jacked up her rent, and one night Jean-Claude casually offered to let her stay with him. For once in her life, she plunged in feetfirst without calculating the risks, and so far, so good.

Tomorrow, Jean-Claude was catching a plane to South Africa for a ten-day photo shoot and she wanted to give him a proper send-off.

Dinner 2 nite. My treat. Bernadette's, she texted. *Fingers X we'll have something big to celebrate.*

She waited a moment to see if he would text back right away. When he didn't, she logged on to OpenTable. Since it was early in the week hopefully she could swing a reservation at their favorite restaurant.

OpenTable came back telling her there were no vacancies at her preferred time of eight P.M. but there was a table available at five-thirty. It was pretty early for dinner, but hey, at least she scored a table. She accepted the five-thirty spot through OpenTable, and then on impulse called the restaurant and asked to have a bottle of iced Dom Perignon waiting tableside.

It wasn't every day a girl made creative director at one of the biggest ad agencies in the country.

Her mother was going to be over the moon when she told her.

Only a couple of executive assistants were in the office. She waved hello and headed for the coffee machine. She poured herself a cup, but drank only half of it, not wanting to look jittery when she walked into her boss's office. With a couple of minutes left to kill, she popped into the ladies' room and reapplied her lipstick.

"Why thank you for this opportunity, Michael," she said, practicing accepting the position. "I do appreciate your confidence in me and I promise you won't be disappointed in my performance."

She smiled carefully. Making sure her upper lip hid her slightly crooked front tooth. She'd learned the flaw-camouflaging smile when she was on the beauty pageant circuit. Why hadn't she gotten veneers years ago? Oh yes, they cost a lot. But with this promotion, she could finally afford them now. Jean-Claude had been nagging her to do it.

She straightened her collar that wasn't askew and brushed imaginary lint off her lapel, and gave herself one last appraisal. She wasn't perfect, not by a long shot, but she looked presentable.

"Here we go, Ms. Creative Director," she murmured, and stepped out into the hallway.

Her boss's door stood ajar.

She poked her head into his office.

Michael sat at his desk, scowling at the computer screen. He looked so much like the *Mad Men* character Roger Sterling that he was almost a caricature, although he possessed none of that character's easygoing, flamboyant ways. Personality-wise, he was more like Don Draper, brilliant, but darkly moody.

He glanced up and his scowl deepened.

Her euphoria evaporated. What had upset him? *Bounce. Don't let his mood throw you.* "Am I too early?"

"Come in," he said curtly. "And close the door behind you."

Squaring her shoulders, she stepped into the room and quietly shut the door. Michael did not ask her to sit down. In fact, he stood up.

Her stomach pitched.

"Jill Jones called me over the weekend," he said.

Jill Jones represented Mowry and Poltish, a chemical company looking to rebrand their image. She and Ms. Jones had had a difference of opinion over the direction of the recent ad campaign, but Melody believed they'd ironed out their differences.

"Isn't Jill sharp? I'm learning so much from her." She

struggled to keep her tone neutral. Where was this going?

"Jill's asked that you be removed from the campaign."

What? Melody gulped. "May I ask why?"

He leaned forward, placed both palms flat on his desk in an intimidating gesture. "She says your values aren't consistent with Mowry and Poltish's vision."

She sank her hands on her hips. Yes, she wanted this promotion more than anything in the world, but she had to set the record straight. "Ms. Jones requested a television campaign that essentially claims their new cleaning product is one hundred percent safe. Her idea was to have a mom cleaning a cutting board with their product and then without rinsing the cutting board, cut up raw fruits and vegetables on it and serve the food to her family."

"Sounds to me like you're making a mountain out of a molehill."

"The cleanser should be thoroughly rinsed off. It says so on the labeling. The chemicals could be harmful if ingested."

"Did Jill ask you to make false claims about the product?"

"No, but—"

"It's not your job to police our clients' ethics."

"Yes, but such a—"

"How many times do I have to tell you we're selling the sizzle not the steak? Advertising is about playing on people's emotions, not about bald-faced facts."

"I know that, which is precisely why I objected to Ms. Jones's vision of the ad. Her version would make people feel safe, but it's a false sense of security and I pointed this out. She agreed to allow the actress playing the TV mom to thoroughly wash the cutting board before cutting food up on it. I don't see—"

"That's just it. You don't *see*."

"See what?"

He shook his head. "Jill says you're difficult."

A heavy weight settled on her shoulders. She was *not* about to get that promotion after all. In fact, she was being called on the carpet. "So being ethical means I'm difficult?"

"Jill didn't ask you to tell a lie."

She extended her arms out to her sides, palms up. "So I shouldn't have said anything?"

"Never argue with a client."

"Even if I believe the ad they want intentionally misleads the consumer?"

"The truth is rubbery, especially in advertising, and you should know that. There's nothing wrong with bending the truth as far as it will go as long as you don't break it."

"You're telling me that you want me to lie?"

"That's not what I said." He stalked around the desk to stare her down. "The fact that you can't tell the difference between a lie and a creative spin on the truth concerns me."

A hot blast of adrenaline shot through her. Stunned, she curled her hands into fists. "What are you saying?"

"This isn't the first time your provincial *ethics*"—he spat the word with disdain—"have tripped up a campaign."

Taken aback, she placed a palm to her chest. "Specifically, what campaigns are you speaking of?"

"The Palmer campaign for one thing."

"But I only worked on the Palmer ad for a few days," she protested.

"Exactly. Palmer said you were argumentative so I put you on another project."

"I merely pointed out that the campaign they wanted was lewd and suggestive. The insinuation of a ménage à trois featuring their garden hoses was in poor taste."

"And yet, that ad went on to become Palmer's most successful campaign ever. Implied sex sold those garden hoses like hotcakes."

"It also garnered more consumer complaints than any other ad we've ever produced."

"Which goes to prove controversy is a good thing. You seemed to understand that when you first came to work here. The family feud television spot you created for Frosty Bites was not only hilarious, but it was one of Tribalgate's most successful campaigns in the last decade."

"So what's the problem?"

"That campaign was six years ago. What have you done for us lately?"

"I won a Clio two years ago!"

"Which means absolutely nothing. The ad you won the Clio for was cute and attention-getting, but in the end it did nothing to increase the sales of the cars it was advertising. And Hyundai dropped Tribalgate over it."

"All right." She nodded. "I see your point. Message received. I will strive to get over my ethics and infuse ads with more titillation."

He shook his head. "I'm sorry, but no you won't."

"You don't want me to put more sexuality in the ads?"

"You will no longer be putting anything into the ads."

"I . . . I don't understand."

"It's not your fault." His tone softened. "You come from a small town. You're just not sophisticated enough for Tribalgate."

Her jaw dropped. "What do you mean? I've lived in the city for twelve years, almost half my life."

"Ms. Spencer, Melody . . ."

Goose bumps spread over her arm. The left muscle in her eye jumped, a tic she got whenever she was super stressed. This couldn't be happening. "What are you saying?"

"Not to sound like Donald Trump or anything, but you're fired."

Stunned, she stood there, mouth open. She caught sight of Michael's desk calendar Tuesday, April 1. April Fool's Day. Relief washed over her.

"Oh, very funny, sir." She smiled circumspectly, hiding that defective tooth. "You almost had me going there."

He glowered. "What are you talking about?"

"I've got to hand it to you. It's the best April Fool's joke anyone has ever played on me."

Slowly, he shook his head. "This is not a joke."

The dread was back and heavier than ever. Oh shit. "This isn't a prank?"

"No."

"Are you sure Ashton Kutcher isn't going to jump out of the closet and declare I've been punked?" she asked hopefully, even as she knew she was well and truly sunk.

No joke. He was serious. She'd been fired.

Her boss held out his palm. "Please hand me your identification badge."

Pressing her lips into a straight line, she fumbled with the ID badge clipped to her lapel. She could barely see through the mist of tears welling up in her eyes, but she refused to let him see her cry. She swallowed the saltiness, blinked hard, and passed her badge to him.

Michael took her ID that represented her entire sense of self, stared at someone over her shoulder, and nodded.

She turned and for the first time saw the two security guards standing in the doorway behind her.

"They'll take you to your desk to collect your things," Michael intoned. "After that, they'll escort you from the building. I'd appreciate it if you didn't cause a scene."

About the Author

LORI WILDE is the *New York Times* and *USA Today* bestselling author of more than seventy works of romantic fiction. She is a two-time RITA award nominee, a four-time *Romantic Times* Reviewers' Choice nominee, and has won numerous other awards. She earned a bachelor's degree in nursing from Texas Christian University and holds a certificate in nursing forensics. An animal lover, Lori is owned by several pets and lives in Texas with her husband, Bill.

Visit www.AuthorTracker.com for exclusive information on your favorite HarperCollins authors.

Give in to your impulses . . .
Read on for a sneak peek at four brand-new
e-book original tales of romance
from Avon Books.
Available now wherever e-books are sold.

THE LAST WICKED SCOUNDREL
A SCOUNDRELS OF ST. JAMES NOVELLA
By Lorraine Heath

BLITZING EMILY
A LOVE AND FOOTBALL NOVEL
By Julie Brannagh

SAVOR
A BILLIONAIRE BACHELORS CLUB NOVEL
By Monica Murphy

IF YOU ONLY KNEW
A TRUST NO ONE NOVEL
By Dixie Lee Brown

An Excerpt from

THE LAST WICKED SCOUNDREL
A Scoundrels of St. James Novella
by Lorraine Heath

New York Times and *USA Today* bestselling author
Lorraine Heath brings us the eagerly awaited
final story in the Scoundrels of St. James series.

Winnie, the Duchess of Avendale, never knew
peace until her brutal husband died. With
William Graves, a royal physician, she's discovered
burning desire—and the healing power of love.
But now, confronted by the past she thought she'd
left behind, Winnie must face her fears . . . or risk
losing the one man who can fulfill all her dreams.

After last night, she'd dared to hope that she meant something special to him, but they were so very different in rank and purpose. She considered suggesting that they go for a walk now, but she didn't want to move away from where she was. So near to him. He smelled of sandalwood. His jaw and cheeks were smooth. He'd shaved before he came to see her. His hair curled wildly about his head, and she wondered if he ever tried to tame it, then decided he wouldn't look like himself without the wildness.

With his thumb, he stroked her lower lip. His blue eyes darkened. She watched the muscles of his throat work as he swallowed. Leaning in, he lowered his mouth to hers. She rose up on her toes to meet him, inviting him to possess, plunder, have his way. She became lost in the sensations of his mouth playing over hers, vaguely aware of his twisting her around so they were facing each other. As she skimmed her hands up over his shoulders, his arms came around her, drawing her nearer. He was a man of nimble fingers, skilled hands that eased hurts and injuries and warded off death. He had mended her with those hands, and now with his lips he was mending her further.

Suddenly changing the angle of his mouth, he deepened

the kiss, his tongue hungrily exploring, enticing her to take her own journey of discovery. He tasted of peppermint. She could well imagine him keeping the hard candies in his pocket to hand to children in order to ease their fears. Snitching one for himself every now and then.

He folded his hands around the sides of her waist and, without breaking his mouth from hers, lifted her onto the desk. Parchment crackled beneath her. She knew she should be worried that they were ruining the plans for the hospital, but she seemed unable to care about anything beyond the wondrous sensations that he was bringing to life.

Avendale had never kissed her with such enthusiasm, such resolve. She felt as though William were determined to devour her, and that it would be one of the most wondrous experiences of her life.

Hiking her skirts up over her knees, he wedged himself between her thighs. Very slowly, he lowered her back to the desk until she was sprawled over it like some wanton. On the desk! She had never known this sort of activity could occur anywhere other than the bed. It was wicked, exciting, intriguing. Surely he didn't mean to do more than kiss her, not that she was opposed to him going further.

She'd gone so long without a caress, without being desired, without having passions stirred. She felt at once terrified and joyful while pleasure curled through her.

As he dragged his mouth along her throat, he began undoing buttons, giving himself access to more skin. He nipped at her collarbone, circled his tongue in the hollow at her throat. She plowed her fingers through his golden locks, relishing the soft curls as they wound around her fingers.

More buttons were unfastened. She sighed as he trailed his mouth and tongue along the upper swells of her breasts. Heat pooled deep within her. She wrapped her legs around his hips, taking surcease from the pressure of him against her. He moaned low, more a growl than anything as he pressed a kiss in the dip between her breasts.

God help her, but she wanted to feel his touch over all of her.

Peeling back her bodice, he began loosening the ribbons on her chemise. In the distance, someplace far far away, she thought she heard a door open.

"The count—" Her butler began and stopped.

"Winnie?" Catherine's voice brought her crashing back to reality.

An Excerpt from

BLITZING EMILY
A Love and Football Novel
by *Julie Brannagh*

All's fair in Love and Football . . .

Emily Hamilton doesn't trust men. She's much
more comfortable playing the romantic lead
in front of a packed house onstage than in her
own life. So when NFL star and alluring ladies'
man Brandon McKenna acts as her personal
white knight, she has no illusions that he'll
stick around. However, a misunderstanding
with the press throws them together in a
fake engagement that yields unexpected (and
breathtaking) benefits in the first installment
of Julie Brannagh's irresistible new series.

Emily had barely enough time to hang up the cordless and flip on the TV before Brandon wandered down the stairs.

"Hey," he said, and he threw himself down on the couch next to her.

His blond curls were tangled, his eyes sleepy, and she saw a pillowcase crease on his cheek. He looked completely innocent, until she saw the wicked twinkle in his eyes. Even in dirty workout clothes, he was breathtaking. She wondered if it was possible to ovulate on demand.

"I'm guessing you took a nap," she said.

"I was supposed to be watching you." He tried to look penitent. It wasn't working.

"Glad to know you're making yourself comfortable," she teased.

He stretched his arm around the back of the couch.

"Everything in your room smells like flowers, and your bed's great." He pulled up the edge of his t-shirt and sniffed it. Emily almost drooled at a glimpse of his rock-hard abdomen. Evidently, it was possible to have more than a six pack. "The guys will love my new perfume. Maybe they'll want some makeup tips," he muttered, and grabbed for the remote Emily left on the coffee table.

He clicked through the channels at a rapid pace.

"Excuse me. I had that." She lunged for it. No such luck. Emily ended up sprawled across his lap.

"The operative word here, sugar, is 'had.'" He held it up in the air out of her reach while he continued to click. He'd wear a hole in his thumb if he kept this up. "No NFL Network." She tried to sit up again, which wasn't working well. Of course, he was chuckling at her struggles. "Oh, I get it. You're heading for second base."

"Hardly." Emily reached over and tried to push off on the other arm of the couch. One beefy arm wrapped around her. "I'm not trying to do anything. Oh, whatever."

"You know, if you want a kiss, all you have to do is ask."

She couldn't imagine how he managed to look so innocent while smirking.

"I haven't had a woman throw herself in my lap for a while now. This could be interesting," he said.

Emily's eyebrows shot to her hairline. "I did not throw myself in your lap."

"Could've fooled me. Which one of us is—"

"Let go of me." She was still trying to grab the remote, without success.

"You'll fall," he warned.

"What's your point?"

"Here." He stuck the remote down the side of the couch cushion so Emily couldn't grab it. He grasped her upper arms, righted her with no effort at all, and looked into her eyes. "All better. Shouldn't you be resting, anyway?"

Emily tried to take a breath. Their bodies were frozen. He held her, and she gazed into his face. His dimple appeared, vanished, appeared again. She licked her lips with the microscopic amount of moisture left in her mouth. He was fighting a smile, but even more, he dipped his head toward her. He was going to kiss her.

"Yes," she said.

Her voice sounded weak, but it was all she could do to push it out of lungs that had no air at all. He continued to watch her, and he gradually moved closer. Their mouths were inches apart. Emily couldn't stop looking at his lips. After a few moments that seemed like an eternity, he released her and dug the remote from the couch cushion. She felt a stab of disappointment. He had changed his mind.

"Turns out you have the NFL Network, so I think I can handle another twenty-four hours here," he announced as he stopped on a channel she'd never seen before.

"You might not be here another twenty-four minutes. Don't you have a TV at home?" She wrapped her arms around her midsection. She wished she could come up with something more witty and cutting to say. She was so sure he would kiss her, and then he hadn't.

An Excerpt from

SAVOR
A Billionaire Bachelors Club Novel
by Monica Murphy

New York Times bestselling author
Monica Murphy concludes her sexy
Billionaire Bachelors Club series with a fiery
romance that refuses to be left at the office.

Bryn James can't take much more of being invisible
to her smart, sexy boss, Matthew DeLuca.
Matt's never been immune to his gorgeous
assistant's charms, and though he's tried to
stay professional, Bryn—with a jaw-dropping
new look—is suddenly making it very difficult.
And when the lines between business and
pleasure become blurred, he'll be faced with
the biggest risk of his career—and his heart.

Bryn

"I shouldn't do this." He's coming right at me, one determined step after another, and I slowly start to back up, fear and excitement bubbling up inside me, making it hard to think clearly.

"Shouldn't do what?"

I lift my chin, my gaze meeting his, and I see all the turbulent, confusing emotions in his eyes, the grim set of his jaw and usually lush mouth. The man means business—what sort of business I'm not exactly sure, but I can take a guess. Increasing my pace, I take hurried backward steps to get away from all that handsome intensity coming at me until my butt meets the wall.

I'm trapped. And in the best possible place too.

"You've been driving me fucking crazy all night," he practically growls, stopping just in front of me.

I have? I want to ask, but I keep my lips clamped tight. He never seems to notice me, not that I ever really want him to. Or at least, that's what I tell myself. That sort of thing usually brings too much unwanted attention. I've dealt with that sort of trouble before, and it nearly destroyed me.

The more time I spend with my boss though, the more I want him to see me. Really see me as a woman. Not the dependable, efficiently organized Miss James who makes his life so much easier.

I want Matt to see me as a woman. A woman he wants.

Playing with fire. . .

The thought floating through my brain is apt, considering the potent heat in Matt's gaze.

"I don't understand how I could be, considering I've done nothing but work my tail off the entire evening," I retort, wincing the moment the words leave me. I blame my mounting frustration over our situation. I'm tired, I've done nothing but live and breathe this winery opening for the last few weeks, and I'm ready to go home and crawl into bed. Pull the covers over my head and sleep for a month.

But if a certain someone wanted to join me in my bed, there wouldn't be any sleeping involved. Just plenty of nakedness and kissing and hot, delicious sex . . .

My entire body flushes at the thought.

"And I appreciate you working that pretty tail of yours off for me. Though I'd hate to see it go," he drawls, his gaze dropping low. Like he's actually trying to check out my backside. His flirtatious tone shocks me, rendering me still.

Our relationship isn't like this. Strictly professional is how Matt and I keep it between us. But that last remark was most definitely what I would consider flirting. And the way he's looking at me . . .

Oh. My.

My cheeks warm when he stops directly in front of me. I

can feel his body heat, smell his intoxicating scent, and I press my lips together to keep from saying something really stupid.

God, I want you. So bad my entire body aches for your touch.

Yeah. I sound like those romance novels I used to devour when I had more time to freaking read. I always thought those emotions were so exaggerated. No way could what happens in a romance novel actually occur in real life.

But I'm feeling it. Right now. With Matthew DeLuca. And the way he's looking at me almost makes me think he might be feeling it too.

"So um, h-how have I been driving you crazy?" I swallow hard. I sound like a stuttering idiot, and I'm trying to calm my racing heart but it's no use. We're staring at each other in silence, the only sound our accelerated breathing, and then he reaches out. Rests his fingers against my cheek. Lets them drift along my face.

Slowly I close my eyes and part my lips, sharp pleasure piercing through me at his intimate touch. I curl my fingers against the wall as if I can grab onto it, afraid I might slide to the ground if I don't get a grip and soon. I can smell him. Feel him. We've been close to each other before, but not like this. Never like this.

An Excerpt from

IF YOU ONLY KNEW
A Trust No One Novel
by Dixie Lee Brown

Beautiful and deadly, Rayna Dugan is a force to be reckoned with. But when she must suddenly defend her life against a criminal empire, Rayna knows she needs backup. Ex-cop Ty Whitlock never meant for his former flame to get mixed up in this mess—a mess he feels responsible for. Now he's got only one choice: find Rayna and keep her safe. But that's the easy part. Once he finds her, can he convince her to stay?

He leaned close. "Goddammit, Rayna. You could have been killed." He breathed the words, and the anger in his expression morphed into fear as he grabbed her forearms and gave her a shake.

The deep emotion playing across his face tugged at her heart. His tortured gaze held her transfixed. She searched for the words to fix everything, starting with the way she'd botched their relationship, but some things couldn't be fixed.

She hooked her fingers through his belt loops and drew semicircles on his firmly toned abdomen with her thumbs until she found her voice again. "But I wasn't . . . thanks to you and Ribs."

Ty straightened and glanced upward, away from her face. "I thought I was going to lose you. I *won't* lose you, Rayna." His piercing gaze fastened on her again, and he raised one hand to caress her cheek. "Don't you get it? We're a team. I *need* you, and whether you'll admit it or not, you need me too."

Hope flared within her at his words, followed almost immediately by a spark of anger. "If you truly believed that, you wouldn't be trying to keep me out of the hunt for Andre. If we're such a good team, why not act like one?"

Ty swept a hand across the back of his neck. "I'm not

trying to keep you . . ." He stopped and looked away from her. "Shit. You're right. I wanted you out of it so you'd be safe, and so I could do my job without worrying about you. I still want you to be safe . . . but I'm fairly certain Joe was going to side with you anyway." He swung his gaze back to her, and amusement quirked his lips. "Besides, if he takes you home, you'll just spend all your time worrying about me."

"Oh, you think so?" Rayna raised a quizzical eyebrow. Did he mean it this time? Would he let her help take Andre down, or was he simply putting her off again?

Ty grew serious. "Stay with me, Rayna, and we'll get this guy. He won't know what hit him."

His soft words and the sincerity in his eyes melted her heart and filled her with sadness at the same time. It sounded like he was asking her to stay with him forever, but he'd already made it clear that he wasn't returning to Montana. So where did that leave them? The smart thing to do would be to ask, but her courage failed in the face of what his answer could be. For right now, she wanted to believe he meant forever, but the truth was she wanted him for however long he would have her, and she'd convince him later that he couldn't live without her. Did that make her desperate? So what if it did? She grabbed a fistful of his shirt and pulled him closer as she shook her head slowly. "Try getting rid of me."

A genuine smile lit his eyes, and his head lowered slowly. His lips touched hers in a lingering kiss, warm and promising more. His arms slid around her waist, pulled her in tightly, and he rested his chin on top of her head. She inhaled a deep breath, and her wild heartbeat began to slow. The safety and comfort of his embrace was exactly what she needed, and it was surprisingly easy to surrender herself to his care. Of course, there were still things to do. They had to get Ribs back and his wounds treated, but for now—for just a moment . . .

A shrill siren screeched in the distance, disturbing the peace of Nate's uncle's property. Ty tensed and raised his head, listening, then pulled his gun from its shoulder holster.